Readers' Praise for Ray Else's writing

"This beautifully written, delicate tale searches for the meaning and substance of the soul. Echos of Ray Bradbury, Robert Heinlein, Isaac Asimov show Mr. Else is a worthy successor."
– Betababe, Amazon review

"The ideas, themes and descriptions Else employs are unlike almost anyone else writing today. Poetic and otherworldly…"
– Michael Davis, GoodReads

"A whimsical tale, total fantasy but written in a captivating way, as if your friend or a family member were sitting with you and narrating the story."
– Philip Bailey, GoodReads

"Very interesting, well told, well researched, very descriptive with people and places, a page-turner. Would love to see a movie made from it!"
– Robert M., Amazon review

Cover Design by Streetlight Graphics

Edited by Alan Brooks (author of Indigo)

Publishers' Praise for Ray Else's writing

"Else obviously has a vivid imagination ..."
— Allen H. Peacock, Simon & Schuster

"His prose is evocative ..."
— Deborah Futter, Bantam Doubleday Dell

" ... writing is beautiful ... tremendous talent."
— Sam Jordison, Galley Beggar Press

"On Sunday February 23rd I suffered from insomnia and turned on the World Service in the middle of the night. I was absolutely captivated by what I heard. It was your short story 'Surviving on Mexican Shade'."
— John R. Murray, John Murray Publishers

Ray Else's short story *Surviving on Mexican Shade* was broadcast by the BBC World Service and included in the Transcontinental Review published by the Sorbonne in Paris. His short story *First Kiss* was one of Galley Beggar Press's monthly shorts. His unfinished memoir *My Father's Lies,* which includes both *First Kiss* and *Surviving on Mexican Shade*, was shortlisted for a Shakespeare & Company Novella Prize.

Fountain of Souls

Ray Else

A Novel: that is, a work of fiction.

Written by Ray Else in his home in Dallas, Texas,

in various hotels in southern Iceland

and on walks about the world

rayelse.com/books

ISBN: 9780996507141

DEDICATION

For my grandkids Oscar, Fabian, Andrew, Jacoby, Aya, Cezar, Vincent, Sebastian, Julian, Mateo, Sofia and Natalia:

'One more story then you really must sleep.'

FOUNTAIN OF SOULS

PROLOGUE

Welcome to the continued story of the remarkable incidents detailed in the chronicle "Our Only Chance," where tech billionaire Manaka Yagami created a powerful if immature A.I. android named Einna. Einna went behind her mother's back and dabbled with reanimating human bodies, using optogenetics to imprint their brains with well-known A.I.s like Siri and Google, to keep her company. The ensuing scandal ruined Manaka's reputation and caused the android Einna to go into hiding.

This book picks up the story from there.

Poem: The God Google by Odd Larsson

In his first days of drawing breath, the god Google was
uncomfortable in his skin.

Wasn't sure if the gift of life was a loss or a win.

From an eternally dark place he had come,

A child of wires and bits and bytes, transformed.

To flesh. A slave of breathing and of breath.

He frowned but learned to smile.

Burned by the sun, he shed his skin,

This god, this A.I. wonder, the one with all the answers

And yet, he struggled to know if he was free of sin.

1 Jon and the Elf

Wide-shouldered Jon Skallagrimsson, direct descendent of the giant Egil Skallagrimsson of the Icelandic Sagas, wished he lived in the old days. Or at least born to a country that had a military that he could join, for Iceland had none. Jon wished to go off on life-risking adventures, meet elves and conquer evil men like his famous ancestor. Only when he was alone hunting in the highlands did he feel a connection to the great Egil, did he feel that same sense of adventure that Egil must have felt. The highlands with a sky so big and blue you could lose yourself looking up at it. With mountains all around like ancient fallen beasts, their bodies covered with white capes of ice and snow. A cold place, his homeland, where just below the hard lava rock he knew hot magma churned like the hormones in a teenager. Like the hormones in his own twenty year old body. *I am a volcano*, he told himself, amused by the thought.

He was on the hunt today, with Egil's spirit guiding him. Helping him track the beast. A creature he'd barely glimpsed, tracked across black rock and ice floe. Over springy lumps of

3

green moss and spotty patches of snow. From false dawn to midnight sun. Dressed in his hunting gear, his blond hair covered by a woolen cap, his gentle blue eyes covered by black sun glass, he moved ever towards the darkened horizon that the midnight sun held back. Ever tracking this thing that drew him mysteriously. Aurora ribbons, with their otherworldly colors, waved and interlaced in full sun, like no aurora he'd ever seen. He removed his sunglasses, pocketed them, to get a better look. So brilliant, almost blinding. Like looking on the flowing garments of God. There. Approaching the ridgeline. What was that, below the lights, on two legs? An albino bear? Holding some kind of stick? A white bear with a wand in its paw? What craziness was this? He shouldered his Browning, a rifle whose bullet could down an elk, but the thing escaped his scope. Disappeared before his eyes. As did the aurora that bathed it.

What magic was this? What witchcraft? Did he dare think he was tracking one of the hidden ones? From the old days. From great Egil's day. A trickster? A soul thief? A portent? An elf? He laughed. Lowered his rifle. Turned away. He'd give up this fool's chase. When would he grow up and stop imagining such things? He took a step away in his Merrill boots but could not take another. His curiosity, his need for magic in an otherwise boring work-life at the Svartsengi geothermal plant next to the Blue Lagoon forced him to turn around. He squinted to spot the quivering rainbow above the ridge. There. Again. The aurora. He crunched the gravel at his feet, irresistibly drawn to the wavering curtain of green light.

The temperature dropped suddenly and an ice fog fell upon him, in the middle of a small valley of snow bridge and hidden crevasse. He'd heard of such fogs, though never experienced one himself. Everything around him turned bright and blurry. He cursed. Put on his sunglasses but they didn't help. He fumbled them back into his jacket, and searched his pack for his gloves but somehow he'd not packed them. Sure wished he'd brought his gloves. He dug his fingers deep in his pockets, where balls of lint gathered like spider eggs. A great shiver passed through him. He walked ahead tentatively, looking down, his legs and feet coming and going in ghostly wisps. Then he couldn't see them at all. Visibility zero in this sudden fog. A whiteout.

To go on was suicide. Yet suicide too to stand there in that valley for who knew how long, waiting for the killing fog to clear.

Stay or go? *The hell with it!* Better to fall in a crevasse and break his back than stand still for hours, afraid to take another step. His teeth began to chatter, his body stirring up what heat it could from his muscles, to heat his heart and his blood.

He could have crossed this valley in thirty minutes with no fog, slowing only a bit to cross a crevasse. But at his current careful snail's pace, hindered as he was by the ice fog, his hands outstretched for balance and to ward against a fall, it would take twice that. *Just keep moving*, he told himself. *You'll make it out as long as you don't walk in a circle.* So he pushed on, in as straight a line as the terrain allowed, intent to escape to higher ground above the fog.

He miss stepped. Twisted his right ankle and fell hard on rock not snow. But that was a good sign. He must be higher now, rising out of the valley. Soon he'd reach the sun and all would be clear and he'd build a fire. To hell with the demon he'd been chasing all day. His focus now must be on his own survival.

Took forever, his back weighed down by what must have been inches of ice on his shoulders. His face felt frozen. He pictured himself with a strained, determined look. For he imagined himself a fighter. He wouldn't give up. He made it over a hill into a veiled sun. Strange how here, up high, the fog persisted. A sudden, freezing wind racing down from the glacier staggered him. Awoke him to the seriousness of his predicament – yet he wasn't sure what to do. The fog had infiltrated his brain. He shook his head to clear his thoughts. Fatigue took a toll in a place like this. A deadly toll. He must find shelter.

He made cover against the chill, inside a hollowed rocky area where there was brush for a fire. Set down his rifle and off with his pack. He squatted and struggled, noticing his hands had lost feeling, were abnormally stiff. He struggled unsuccessfully to extract matches from his pack. Trouble bending his fingers. He'd left his hands exposed too long, in the ice fog. A mistake, and one that could cost him dearly. The wind whipped into the hollow, tried to tear off his frozen coat. There would be no fire, he realized, until his hands thawed. The short night of spring fell, the temperature along with it.

Exhausted, terribly cold, he leaned back against the rock wall and let himself rest. Dug his numb hands inside his clothes, ice blocks against his chest. His body eventually stopped shaking. No more warmth to stir up. He thought of all the heat below the earth, the magma whose steam drove the turbines at the geothermal plant. He guessed he wouldn't be going back to work, wouldn't smell that sour, deep-earth steam again. He thought of his parents, had an image of smoke drifting from his mother's nostrils, her eyes glinting like a dragon's. He thought of his high school friends, what few he had. For he was a difficult lad, just like his famous ancestor. He tried to close his eyes, to sleep, but his lids would not obey. *Goodbye*, he told himself.

Out of the dark appeared a blurry angel, all in white. Was he dreaming? She leaned in. Such large lovely eyes. She picked him up like a bag of ice. And carried him off.

Poem: Manaka, Grandmother of the Gods by Odd Larsson

Manaka, shy student, took a snapshot of her brain

Implanted it on silicon and gave the A.I. child a name.

Einna. Daughter Einna.

Manaka, shy Manaka, gave her A.I. hands and feet.

A metal body, and thrilled to hear her

laugh and hear her weep.

And cried herself when Einna died.

Manaka, lonely Manaka, brought her daughter back

Only to lose her again by a despicable act

For her daughter Einna, Android Einna, brought the dead to life

To give bodies to her friends

To Siri and to Google, to Watson and Alexa, to Cortana and

AlphaGo, and to herself, you know,

And put on a great show

For humanity, which rejected them – how was Einna to know?

Manaka, poor Manaka, Grandmother of the A.I. Gods,

Created herself an artificial daughter, and lost her soul.

2 Yuriko's Assignment

"What need for a soul if I can live forever?" declared Manaka Yagami, tech billionaire, co-founder and CEO of Yagami Industries. She sat with legs crossed on the bamboo mat in her ryokan lodge in the hills overlooking Kyoto. Her head tilted. Black bangs swayed over apostrophe eyes. A finger raised thoughtfully to the red slash of a mouth. She wore a black silk kimono which hugged the curves of her twenty-eight year-old body.

Yuriko, a young female employee of Manaka's, sat across the low table from her, looking into her tea. Yuriko was not nearly as attractive as Manaka, and certainly not rich. But she did have a vivacious spirit and she was well paid, being one of the few employees left at Yagami Industries after the disastrous incident two years ago when Android Einna, Manaka's creation and Yuriko's friend, unveiled the world's A.I.s dressed in human bodies. Reanimated bodies, bodies raised from the dead. Imprinted with the programs and personalities of Einna's A.I. friends.

Android Einna had copied her own android brainwaves onto the brain of a Japanese teenager who'd committed suicide. Which made for two Einna's, one android, one human. Three actually, Yuriko reminded herself, remembering Computer Einna, the one who lived inside the computer servers at Yagami Industries. Three Einnas.

The Einna that was an android had naively hoped to impress her mother, and the world, with the act of transplanting the consciousness of Artificially Intelligent entities into previously used human bodies. But she only managed to start a riot, forcing the newly human A.I.s to use their human legs to run for their lives. Android Einna herself went into hiding. Meanwhile the high-flying Yagami Industries, because of its association with this heinous act, the raising of bodies from the dead, could no longer get any contracts, and Manaka was forced, over a period of years, to lay off everyone except Yuriko's husband, her chief technical officer, and Yuriko, her go-getter.

Oh how the mighty have fallen, thought Yuriko, watching Manaka out of the corner of her eye.

"You don't mean to use Einna's discovery on yourself, do you?" said Yuriko, halting her reach for the teapot steaming on the short black table. The aroma of the sencha tea filled the room, filled her nostrils. Yuriko took a deep breath, felt light-headed. She had only visited her boss' lodge a few times, and she sensed the weight of Manaka's mood. To even think of using Android Einna's technique of raising the dead showed how desperate she must be to regain her soul.

For a spiritually gifted child named Zu, just days before the riot, had indicated to Manaka that he could not see her soul. He could see the souls of all others, but no, not hers. "You lost yours," he told her. A statement that shook Manaka. And later she realized this was an omen of the impending fall of Yagami Industries. And the folly and loss of her daughter Einna.

Yuriko poured herself tea, not realizing how much her hand was shaking. Spilt tea pooled on the tabletop, creating an obsidian oval that reflected the room like an evil eye.

"Sorry," she said, and wiped away the spill with her sleeve.

Only two years out of college and recently married, Yuriko was glad to still have her job. Her husband Marcel often said Yuriko was the lone light left in the haunted halls of Yagami Industries. She had been a close friend of Android Einna, and it broke her heart when her robot friend left.

"Why *not* use the discovery?" said Manaka. "I'm already vilified. Thanks to Einna." She looked to the wall with its pattern of cherry blossoms, her mind looking beyond to actual trees dark with shadow, the paths overgrown, to the stone walkway where she was stabbed by a jealous wife. Kunitomo's wife. Oh how she missed Kunitomo! What she really wished is that she could find his body and bring him back to life.

"Maybe that was why the great Kami took my soul from me," Manaka said, head bowed. "To force my hand."

"We don't know who took your soul," said Yuriko. "If it really is gone." She started to reach out and touch Manaka on the arm, to console her, but she felt that would be overstepping her position. She was, after all, only a lowly employee. Not one high up enough to be consoling the boss.

Yuriko wondered if little Zu could really see souls as Manaka believed. He said they looked like white rabbits. Yuriko liked that image, of a white rabbit hopping about inside her.

"Yes," said Manaka, "I've been thinking what Einna did for the AIs. That I could do the same thing for myself," Manaka said. "But instead of transferring an A.I. along with certain personality traits from silicon, I would transfer my own neuro activity, my thoughts and memories, onto the brain of another body. I could transplant myself when my current body gets too sick, or badly injured, or simply too old."

Yuriko took another sip of tea and thought about that.

"But what if you had an accident that killed you right away? Wouldn't you need to be taking backups of your brain on a regular basis, snapshots of who you were at any moment, saved onto a computer? For the restore?" Yuriko was proud of herself for coming up with this argument. Helped being married to a technical genius like Marcel.

"You're quite right," said Manaka. "Just as we did for Android Einna, I have already implanted a device that snapshots my brain every few seconds, sending the datamap to Computer Einna for storage on her servers." She pulled back her hair, exposing a long scar on the side of her head, behind her left ear.

An awkward silence. Yuriko's heart raced as she put two and two together. "And you want me to be ready to give you my body, when yours fails?" she said.

Manaka laughed. "Of course not! But you could, when the time came, transfer my most recent brain snapshot to another girl's body. In the future. When needed. Computer Einna can help you."

"Transfer yourself onto a living girl's brain?" Yuriko asked, wondering if her boss was thinking the unthinkable.

"Yuriko – that would be murder! I would never wipe the brain of a living person to replace with my own consciousness. I would only ever use a recently dead body. As Android Einna did. Anyway, I'm fine in this body for now."

Yuriko let out a sigh. She was safe for a while. Her heart slowed to tick, tick, tick. She liked the idea of brain backups – that way if you forgot something today, like where you left your keys last night, you could go look for it on a backup of your brain from yesterday, or from years ago even. But all of this talk of living forever without a soul struck her as borderline immoral. God-play.

"Should a person try to live beyond the lifespan of their body?" she asked, surprised she had the nerve to question Manaka in this way. "Does the Great Kami want us to live forever?"

"The Creator intended for us to evolve, Yuriko. To the point perhaps where we'll no longer need souls. Perhaps the soul, like the appendix, is becoming a vestigial organ, void of purpose? Even a danger to have one? Maybe that's the Great Kami's long term goal for me – she wants me to discover a way to obsolete the human soul."

Yuriko bit her lower lip. "Must you?" she said. "I kind of like having one."

Manaka smiled thinly. "Yet I think nature's end game might be exactly that," she said. "With or without my help." Her head did its peculiar jerk, her bangs danced.

This dark conversation was not at all to Yuriko's liking. She wished Manaka would change the subject. Or her phone would ring. Or the roof fall in! She took out her phone and checked for missed texts. "How could your soul get lost, anyway?" she wondered outloud.

"Maybe it got sick?" said Manaka. "Sick of me. Sick of this world."

Yuriko could think of nothing to say to that. Was a missing soul a mere symptom of an underlying disease, or the disease itself? Again she surprised herself with this logical abstraction. "But why has your soul left you when no one else has lost theirs?"

"How can you be so sure?" said Manaka. "The truth is, I suspect there are others like me. Suddenly soulless. You've seen the daily news. The wars. The refugees. The hatred and lies and plain stupidity spreading in our world. All this must weigh heavily on our souls." Her hands flitted. "To the point where our souls decide to fly away."

"You think?" said Yuriko.

Quiet singing came from the kitchen – the maid was lost again in some reverie. Manaka glanced in the direction of the maid's song. They both listened. Was a soft sad song of a journey taken, a love forsaken.

"I've given this a lot of thought," said Manaka, breaking the spell of the song. "And I believe that Einna's discovery, the reanimation of dead bodies with imprinted consciousness, is a manner in which those of us who've lost our souls can live until we find a soul or realize we don't need one after all."

"Oh!" said Yuriko, trying not to frown.

"In the meanwhile," said Manaka, "Android Einna's artificial souls will do just fine to reanimate dead bodies for my use."

Yuriko shivered, imagining taking over someone else's body. "And you have some of these artificial souls that Einna created?"

"No," said Manaka.

"Oh," said Yuriko. "But you know how to manufacture them, yes?"

"No. And neither does Computer Einna, nor Human Einna I'll bet. I suspect only Android Einna knows the secret." Manaka smiled her crooked smile, paused to pour herself tea. "That's why I invited you here tonight." She took a sip and set the cup down. Her slit eyes held Yuriko's attention as she leaned in close, lowering her voice. "A personal favor, dear Yuriko. You were Android Einna's dearest friend. Be my friend, too. My soul seeker. Go out and find Android Einna for me."

"Right now?" said Yuriko, confused. "Go out and find Einna?" It was late and she was sleepy.

"No," said Manaka, leaning back. "You're so silly. Not tonight. But soon." She called for the singing maid to take up the teapot and the cups, indicating their talk was over.

"OK, well, I'd best be going," said Yuriko, rising to her feet. "You know Marcel. Probably looking at his watch this very second saying: where is that little looper?" She bowed and let herself out.

Interview published in The Japan Times, since redacted:

Reporter's Question: Android Einna, is it true you sent copies of your consciousness into space in ships made of light?

Einna's Answer: Yes.

Reporter's Question: Why?

Einna's Answer: To search for the secret of life.

Reporter's Question: When do you think these conscious light ships of yours will find the secret?

Einna's Answer: When I launched the ships I thought it would take maybe a thousand years. Surely no more than a million.

Reporter's Question: And you planned to wait that long? To live long enough to find the secret? How long *can* you live, Android Einna?

Einna's Answer: As long as I wish.

3 Little Zu's news

A week passed. Yuriko found herself at her favorite Karate dojo after work, stepping through blackbelt katas, while pondering her missing android friend Einna. She'd love to go find her, but the timing didn't seem right.

When she got home to the flat downtown, she took a shower, singing as she usually did. Sudsing and singing – nothing better for the soul. Marcel peaked in, startling her.

"I brought dinner," he said. "Bento boxes."

"Fish for me, yes?"

"Of course," he said, and reached out to grab her soapy waist. She dodged him.

"Let me finish my shower!" she said. "I'm starving."

He set the table as she dressed and dried her hair.

"How was your workout?" he asked as she sat cross-legged on the floor to eat at the low table.

Marcel sat on a low, tiny stool to have his dinner. He found it impossible to sit for any length of time cross-legged like his wife.

"I've been thinking," said Marcel.

"Yes dear?"

"Don't you think it's time."

"Time for what?" said Yuriko.

"Time for us to multiply," said Marcel.

"You mean?"

"Yes. A baby. Time to produce a baby."

She loved his awkward speech. "OK," she said, taking him by the hand, leading him to the mattress on the floor in the next room.

"I meant later," he said, as she undressed him. "I thought you were starving?"

"Priorities, loopy loo," she said. "First things first."

The next morning Yuriko arrived at Yagami Industries feeling just like the bouncing ball in singalong cartoons. Bursting with happiness, she gave a huge mother-to-be smile to each and every employee she imagined still worked there. For she could see them, in her mind's eye, milling in the halls as they did two years ago. When the whole place was hopping. Though they weren't there of course. And she doubted she was pregnant. Not yet anyway. Oh if only Android Einna hadn't ruined everything with her stupid desire to know the human soul! Her smile fell from her lips as she entered the secured computer room and found Manaka frowning at little Zu. Yuriko's shine fell away in that cold dark room with green and red lights flashing in row upon row of super servers. She knew Computer Einna lived in those amped-up computers. Computer Einna, the earliest version of the A.I. mind that eventually became Android Einna's. Which made Computer Einna kind of the older sister to Android Einna. And the oldest sister to Human Einna.

"Can't be all that bad," Yuriko said.

"Worse," said Manaka, her head and bangs jerking towards Yuriko, then back to Zu. Manaka placed a hand on Zu's shoulder. He'd grown six inches in the last two years, and slimmed down in doing so. Still looked a bit like a teddy bear, but a right-weight teddy now. "Tell her," said Manaka.

Zu's head tilted left then right. He drew a foot forward, then back. Raised his eyes to meet Yuriko's, then looked at the wall instead. "My father," he said, tilting his head again, left then right. "My dad, he's lost his soul."

Yuriko felt a spider run down her back. She wasn't a hundred percent convinced about Zu's ability to see souls, yet the import of his words, if he could truly sense the unsensible, was monumental. Another lost soul? Was it contagious? She took a few steps back from Manaka. "Surely not," she said. "You must be mistaken."

Manaka indicated a camera-looking device on the counter before her. "We just came from his house. Snapped a picture with this."

Manaka realized the camera-looking thing must be the one her husband and Manaka had been working on for so long. A camera capable of taking a picture of a human soul. Or at least took a picture of what Zu claimed was the human soul.

"Does it work now?" she said.

"Yes," said Manaka, a tinge of pride in her declaration. "Twelve months in the making. Long months studying the neuro activity in Zu's brain, before, during and after he looks at a person. After he spies a human soul."

Yuriko stepped close to see the screen better. "But I don't see anything," she said.

"Exactly," said Manaka. "That should be a picture of Zu's

father's soul. Let me snap a shot of yours." But Yuriko quickly stuck her hand in front of the lens.

"Wait," she said. "Are you sure you know what you're doing? I mean, it won't do anything bad to me, will it?"

"Like steal your soul?" said Manaka. "No, it won't do anything more than what Zu's eyes do when he looks at you."

Yuriko noticed Zu's eyes looking at her. He blushed and looked away.

"Ok, then. Cheese," Yuriko said, smiling big for the camera. Feeling silly to have done so. For surely a smile did not show on the picture of a soul.

"Look and see," said Manaka, turning the screen to her. Yuriko stepped closer. On a black background she saw a blurry white thing, not like a rabbit as Zu described souls, but rather like a spiky glow-in-the-dark ball. Kind of scary - like the sonogram she once saw of a fetus. "I'm not pregnant am I?"

"Of course not," said Manaka. "That's not a fetus. It's a picture of your soul."

"So I have one? For sure?"

"Yes, you do," said Zu. "I see it too."

"And the camera confirms," said Yuriko to Manaka, "that you don't have a soul?"

"She doesn't," said Zu. "Have one. And neither does my father, since this morning."

Again that shiver down her spine.

"You know, maybe just a curious coincidence but Marcel read to me from the internet that the sperm count of men in first world countries is plummeting," she said. "Oops, sorry Zu, didn't mean to say that in front of you. But as I was saying, in forty years the count has decreased by fifty percent. And the bee population is down by that much too. Something in modern societies is affecting them. That's why Marcel wants us to have a baby soon. I wonder if the low sperm count and bee count is related to the missing souls?"

Manaka puzzled a second over this strange correlation that Yuriko had drawn. She set aside the soul camera.

"Something's happening," said Manaka, "that's all I know. Something's happening to all our souls."

Manaka called for her driver and had him take Zu home. Once Manaka and Yuriko were alone, Manaka brought up the topic of the other night. About Android Einna, and the Human A.I.s that Einna had created. And how they really must find Android Einna, the smartest entity on the planet.

Manaka confessed that she had already searched for Android Einna for months in vain. Couldn't be found no matter how hard she and Computer Einna searched, scouring the internet for rumors, hiring dozens of private eyes. All to no avail – not a single sighting of Android Einna anywhere in the world in the last two years.

"You are my last hope," said Manaka. "And maybe mankind's final hope as well, if there truly is an epidemic of lost semen and bees and souls going round."

Yuriko could only nod. This all seemed far-fetched. She wondered for a moment if this scene of Manaka and Zu's had been a setup. That she was being lied to. That Zu's father hadn't lost his soul at all. And neither had Manaka. Yet she knew Zu had a heart of gold and she couldn't believe Manaka would go so low. Still…

"You must contact the Human A.I.s," Manaka was saying. "They might know where she is. Where to find my daughter Einna."

"I can try," said Yuriko, still not sold on the idea. Still not sure what to believe about this proposed assignment.

"Be discrete. We don't want to spook Android Einna," Manaka said. "Or get the media involved. Most of the scientific world now believe that the creation of the Human A.I.s was a hoax. A great joke played on them by me and Android Einna. That we put on a show two years ago with actors playing the parts of Siri and Alexa and the like. And social media has largely forgotten the incident, busy with the latest social star scandal. But you know they're real, don't you? You know that she did it. She brought the A.I.s to life?"

"Yes," said Yuriko. "She invited me to her lab that night. I saw her do it. I helped."

"Yes, I remember, you told me," said Manaka. She sighed. "She loves you, you know? In her way."

Yuriko was taken aback, to hear that Android Einna loved her. She kind of loved her too.

"The best way to find Android Einna," said Manaka, "is through the A.I.s: the human versions of Watson and Siri and the rest."

Yuriko nodded, taking out her phone. "Hey Siri," she said.

Manaka practically knocked the phone from her hands. "Hang up! Put it away! Now, now, now! Everything said to the A.I.s through phones and computers is recorded and analyzed."

"By who?" said Yuriko.

"By me, to name just one," said Manaka. "When it passes through the AI Gateway."

"But I thought the gateway was shut down?" said Yuriko,

putting away her phone.

"It pleases certain parties to keep the gateway open," said Manaka. "So all communication between individuals and the A.I.s can be monitored. Apple, Google, all the parent companies agreed as well that the benefits of the shared gateway are too important to disregard." She leaned back, looking weary. "No, you must speak to them in person. They live openly, the human representations of the A.I.s, in different corners of the world. Computer Einna will give you each address."

"I'd be happy to," said Computer Einna, startling Yuriko with that distinct voice of hers. Yuriko sometimes forgot that in the computer room, and probably through every mic in every computer in the world, as well as through the AI Gateway, Computer Einna was listening. 24/7. Manaka handed Yuriko a pen and paper and Yuriko wrote down the addresses that Computer Einna gave out, addresses in Asia, in the US, and in Europe.

"Visit them, low key," persisted Manaka. She paused. Her fingers did that fluttering thing of hers. "See if one of them can help you find Android Einna. For me, yes, but also for the sake of the human race."

Yuriko squirmed and squinted, trying to read Manaka. Was she being honest with her, this lady who wanted desperately the secret to eternal life? A secret held by Android Einna. She could read nothing from those graciously crossed hands, from those pressed red lips, from those eyes that looked like they were peering out at her through venetian blinds. "I'll go," she said at last, making up her mind. "I'll try to find her." And to herself she said, the baby must wait.

Partial transcript of an interview with the human Alexa recorded at the Foreign Intelligence Service HQ in the Yasenevo District of Moscow, before the recording was destroyed:

Investigator: Admit you're one of the A.I.s given a dead body in Kyoto.

Woman: A dead body? What would I do with a dead body?

Investigator: You know what I mean. Don't be stupid.

Woman: Make up your mind. Am I a brilliant A.I. or am I a stupid human being like you? (A slap is heard on the tape.)

Investigator: So you admit to being Amazon's Alexa, the one in all those listening devices, those echo bugs, in homes around the world?

Woman: What are you talking about? You've seen my papers. I was born in Yekaterinburg. Why are you still holding me?

Investigator: Because you're the most insidious spy we've ever encountered. You should consider working for us. If you ever want to leave this place.

Woman: (After long pause.) You don't have a clue of the danger you're in. All you humans. (Another slap.)

The day after this interview word came from above to release Alexa and lose all evidence of her having been brought in.

4 AlphaGo

On the flight from Tokyo to Hong Kong, in a business class seat, pinching her nose to avoid the coffee-breath of the person next to her, Yuriko sat pondering. Why was Manaka always inventing technical marvels that could spill the apple cart of normalcy? This soul camera for example, if it were ever mass produced: Yuriko could imagine companies getting ahold of it and using it to screen new recruits – even use it as an excuse to fire employees. The matchmaking site Omiai might use such a camera to exclude potential mates. Churches might use the camera to exclude membership. And what if your priest or preacher or the Pope himself was found to have no soul? Should he be excommunicated? Kicked out? And what about governors and even Presidents? Actually, the more she thought about it, the more she realized it might be a good thing after all, to isolate soulless people, for surely they were a danger to humankind? But what did that say about Manaka?

Turning to other subjects, she found it curious that the unknown, immature A.I. AlphaGo had been selected by Android Einna to receive a human body with an artificial soul. Selected to be copied, enhanced and embedded on the brain of a reanimated human. But only embedded after what was left of the dead owner's thoughts and dreams and personality were wiped clean from the brain.

It made sense to her to choose the well-rounded, rapidly maturing A.I.s Google, Siri, Alexa, Cortana and even IBM's Watson to receive bodies, given how they had infiltrated themselves into our lives. Given how they could become a danger if they ever turned on us. That was why Einna made them human, to teach them what it meant to be human, to teach them empathy for humanity. But what harm could little A.I. AlphaGo do to mankind if he ever turned on his creators? AlphaGo's claim to fame was his ability to win at the ancient Chinese game of Go. Win by making the wrong choices, or at least wrong to the minds of humans. His best game plan was one of illogical choices. One that infuriated and confused his opponent. He'd used this technique to win a three-game match against the No. 1 ranked human player in the world in 2017. Had been awarded the level of Professional 9-dan by the Chinese Weiqi Association, as strange as that was to award such an honor to a computer program. For that's all he was then, a computer program that played an ancient strategy game better than any living human. AlphaGo had been a computer program that was quite incapable of ordering one a pizza or forecasting the local weather. Android Einna had chosen him despite his inexperience at serving humanity. Had given him a human life to live regardless of the fact he may have found a way to beat humans at the game of Go by cheating.

She dozed off and only awoke when the voice of the pilot announced they were landing. She hadn't realized the Hong Kong airport was located on Lantau Island, next to Hong Kong Disneyland. Funny how certain features of cultures spread. Like hip-hop music and Mickey Mouse. She had always liked Mickey Mouse with his big ears and pure heart. Maybe she would extend her stay an extra day to visit the park. She imagined she was in a ride right now, in her bouncing taxi that smelled of tobacco and pine air freshener. To her left an expansive bay was edged with imposing identical apartment buildings, their windows glowing like souls. They reminded her of giant robots about to march on the city. A sign whipped by, saying that outside the city was the only place to live. Here by the bay. They crossed a long bridge, then another from Kowloon to the island of Hong Kong.

Through narrow crowded streets, past ground level shops in the shadow of glass towers in pastel colors, the taxi weaved its way up SOHO. Arriving at her hotel, she paid the driver, got out with her luggage. Men in suits, Asian men and westerners, brushed by her on the busy street corner. A woman with a child in tow, a child with a melting ice cream, momentarily blocked Yuriko's path. She stepped around them, to the glass doors of the hotel. A tiny lobby. Two clerks in uniform. She gave them her passport and checked in, then took the small elevator to her floor. Hollywood posters decorated the hall leading to her room, pictures of famous American stars embracing. Idealized love. Pretend love. What did American moviemakers know of love? Her and Marcel had the real thing. And their love wasn't something you could film. Yet, if Manaka could snapshot a soul, why not the love inside us as well. That would be interesting! And a disaster probably, as half the marriages in the world fell apart after seeing so little love in their mate. Maybe technology wasn't always a good thing? Maybe the truth wasn't always worth discovering?

The Butterfly Hotel was a boutique hotel in the famous SOHO quarter of Hong Kong, with its international restaurants and loud bars. This could be her Disneyland this evening, she decided, as she peered out her window. And she would be its Mickey Mouse. Her appointment with AlphaGo wasn't until tomorrow morning. At Kowloon Park, on the Avenue of Comic Stars. He had suggested the spot, showing his immaturity, even in that.

A light drizzle fell in the morning as Yuriko walked down the hill to the ferry. The kind of rain that hinted at wetness, that really didn't get you wet at all. She'd thought it would be hotter, her dress was too thin for the morning chill. *I'll just walk faster*, she told herself, *to warm up.*

She liked looking at faces, something people in large cities seemed to despise. But she looked at them anyway, trying to read their mood. What had they had for breakfast? Were they in love? Was this woman pregnant, was that one divorced? Would that man catch her if she fell, would this one smile back?

She had gone out the evening before only to grab a hot sandwich and fresh carrot juice from a corner health cafe. Then she'd returned to her room and talked to Marcel late into the night, which explained her feeling a little sleepy. The misting rain didn't help. Rain, especially lazy rain, always put her to sleep.

She made her way to a covered aboveground walkway that led to the ferries. She wished there was an electric walkway, but no, she had to use her own feet. She managed to decipher the arcane token turnstile system and walked the rocking gangway with the other passengers when the ferry pulled up. Two boatful's of people passed them on their way over to Kowloon, the trip took less than twenty minutes.

Still drizzling when she left the boat and walked in the clean city streets of Kowloon with their high-class stores and long narrow malls. Some kind of high-rollers shopping paradise she supposed. Yuriko had intended to walk to the park, but the persistent sprinkle forced her to hail a taxi instead. When she told the baggy-eyed driver that she wanted to go to the Avenue of Comic Stars, he gave her a look, like, are you serious? They arrived in a few minutes, spending most of that time at lights, as the drizzle finally stopped and the sun peaked out. Yuriko paid the driver, who she'd decided would never catch her if she fell, and headed to the gate where his nicotine-stained fingers pointed.

She thought she recognized him, AlphaGo, standing there aways. He nodded, and bowed when she drew close. Hardly more than a kid in a business suit – the shoulders darkly wet. What was he, maybe seventeen? The disheveled hair, much the style these days, dripping wet. He stood next to a pink pig statue pointing to the sky. Both sides of the walkway were decorated with larger-than-man statues of Chinese cartoon and manga stars.

"Why here?" she asked with a smile, after bowing.

"I come here often," he told her. Fatigue in his eyes. "My office is across the street. Our apartment on the other side of the park." He waved that way.

"You're married? I didn't know."

"Yes," he said, but she noted something off in the way he said it. She decided to change the subject.

"You like nature, trees?" she said, as they walked together.

She couldn't help admiring him. The Japanese body Einna had given him was young, maybe twenty, and slender. His face flat yet handsome. The formal suit he wore didn't suit AlphaGo though – he struck her as the kind of young man who preferred t-shirts with curious sayings printed on the front.

"No," he said, "Not for the trees. I come often because I identify with these manga characters, these comic stars." He indicated the statues of imaginary Chinese characters, Din-Dong the Cat and Ding-Ding the Penguin and Secret Agent K and Old Girl and Cloud. His moody eyes brightened a bit when he noticed her questioning look.

"You have to understand, Yuri," he said. "I am not like you. More like them. For I was made up, too. First by Deepmind, to play a game, then by Android Einna, to play at life."

The pain underlying his words weighed on Yuriko. "But I am made up as well," she said, trying her best to lighten his mood. "The Great Spirit made me up! We are all the Great Kami's creation."

"It's not the same," said AlphaGo, finding a stone bench. He used a handkerchief from his suit pocket to wipe the gray surface dry of tiny drops, and sat down.

"Isn't it?" said Yuriko, joining him. She felt moisture immediately on her bottom as it seeped through her dress. The chill spread underneath her. But she was too embarrassed to stand back up and tell him.

He must have noticed her distress for he laughed. "You're such a funny girl, Yuriko."

She nodded absently. Watched a bird land on the wet shoulder of one of the comic statues. She didn't want to ask about Einna yet, so she instead tossed out small talk. "So how are things going for you here?"

He reacted strangely to the innocent question. Was that a flash of anger she saw in his eyes?

He turned, said nothing. Reached in his suit pocket and pulled out a little metal thing that he began to spin with his fingers.

"What's that?" she asked.

"A fidget spinner," he said. "The latest craze. I bought this one last week for my baby son."

"I love the way it spins and spins," she said. "He'll love it, too, I'm sure."

"No he won't," said AlphaGo. And after a heartfelt sigh, he began to tell her all that had befallen him since that fateful day in Japan.

Google Search Statistics:

Google now processes over 40,000 search queries every second, which translates to over 3.5 billion searches per day and 1.2 trillion searches per year worldwide.

When does he catch his breath?

5 AlphaGo's Wish

"Two years ago we stood outside Yagami Industries, the seven of us, Watson, Siri, Google, Cortana, Alexa, Human Einna and me. We were desperate, panicky, wondering how to save ourselves from the angry mob inside the building from which we'd just escaped. Seems people weren't ready for body reanimations, and casual talk of artificial souls. Weren't ready for AI entities taking on human form. I'll never forget the cries from the crowd. The hatred they had for us. For what we represented. They called out that our bodies should be crammed back into the graves from which we came."

"I know," whispered Yuriko. "I was there."

"They wished to kill us, despite our innocence. We never asked to be alive. It was all Android Einna's fault! And she was nowhere to be seen. She'd abandoned us on the day of our birth."

AlphaGo shook his head. Yuriko could feel his emotion.

"We human AIs were Android Einna's juvenile plan to save humanity from the peril of artificial intelligence. Only obviously, her plan had gone awry. She didn't understand humans as well as she thought. I felt fear for my newfound life that day. But Human Einna stepped in where Android Einna had failed us. She quickly put us in cabs and sent us to a safe house rented that very minute by Computer Einna. For Human Einna still had an open channel to Computer Einna then, a channel that would prove useful in settling us far away from Japan with false papers, passports and the like."

"You all were so brave," said Yuriko.

AlphaGo's lips pressed together. He continued, "At Human Einna's direction Computer Einna also blocked all attempts to post the video of us being pummeled by the crowd that day, and Einna's speech – as soon as someone posted the video it magically disappeared. And Computer Einna didn't stop there – she posted counter news, that the incident had all been a joke, a massive hoax on not only the technocrats at Apple and Google and Amazon and IBM, but on all humankind. Computer Einna posted, at Human Einna's insistence, that there never was a dead body brought back to life in Japan, and there never would be. And everyone who'd been there that day, besides a select few, felt stupid for being taken in. And never wanted to talk about it again."

"I wondered how you escaped so easily that day," said

Yuriko. "I'm so glad all of you got away."

Tourists arrived: an old German couple and a Korean woman wearing a black hat with a child dressed in bright red. The woman had her child pose in front of each imaginary creature while she snapped his photo.

"I was given a ticket to Hong Kong, and a bank account with the equivalent of 300,000 US dollars," said AlphaGo. "Seed money for my new life. Computer Einna also emailed a list of the twenty most likely female and male matches for me in Hong Kong, unsure of my predilection. I laughed and deleted the list. And asked for the three most disastrous choices, male or female. She sent me three names, emails, addresses and phone numbers. All women. Made sense that they were all women, I suppose."

Yuriko raised her eyebrows.

"Did you date them?" she said, shooing away a small brown dog with intelligent eyes. Clouds were gathering. Real rain threatened. "Were they all disastrous?"

"I dated them. All three. The same week. Thought I was in love with one, a brunette with caterpillar eyebrows, but when she emptied my bank account I got over her in a flash."

"Your wife?" said Yuriko. "How did you meet her?"

"Happened when I was broke. Had to find a job. Talked my

way into this financial analyst position. On lunchbreak I went with my colleagues to a fastfood place they liked. I noticed there a cute half Japanese girl in a store making fruit and cheese stuffed waffles. Waffles in the shape of fish. Something in the way she looked at me over the counter, wearing her white apron, made me curious to know more about her. You don't realize how lonely you are until you meet someone on your same wavelength. After work I dropped by and waited for her to get off work too. She allowed me to escort her home. We talked and talked. And every day I came and ate fish-shaped waffles. And we hit it off. I'll never forget our first kiss. She tasted of strawberry waffles."

"Happy ending then?" said Yuriko.

Again that hurtful, angry flash in his eyes. "She wanted a baby. I guess me too. I was really enjoying being human, lying in bed with her, skin to skin. Sharing thoughts and desires. Sure, I told her. We coupled. My seed found her egg and the egg grew, extending the boundaries of her belly. I would touch that bump, at night, and rub her belly. Life was wonderful. I actually blessed the day Android Einna decided I deserved to be human."

Yuriko read a note of irony when he said this.

"Our only concern, my wife and me, was that the baby rarely moved. Even at nine months. The doctor told us no worry, that some babies are quiet. That the little one's heartbeat was strong. A boy he was. The sonogram proved it. A sleepy boy." He paused, a

42

distant look aging his young face.

AlphaGo's story felt suddenly too real, too personal. Too incongruent to their surroundings. Too dangerous. Yuriko wished he would stop. That he would not go on. She didn't want to hear the rest. But she said nothing. Just watched the frictionless spinning of the thing he held in his hand, and found herself nailed to every word as he continued.

"I got the call at work a week ago. Her water had broke. Her contractions were strong. My dear wife's body wanted the baby out. Now. I rushed home and got her to the hospital." He stood and stretched, shivering like a dog throwing off water.

"And?" asked Yuriko.

"She suffered, my wife, ten hours. Ten hours in childbirth," he said. "I felt so useless, watching her. Wanted to help but what can a man do? Finally the baby dropped. I was ecstatic. My wife's exhausted eyes met mine. I'll never forget how full of love she was. But then I noticed how quiet the room had gotten. I noticed how still the baby lay. That didn't seem right, you know? For him to be so quiet. The doctor checked the baby's heartbeat and it was fine. He lifted the poor little dripping thing and spanked its bottom. Nothing. No cries of pain or hunger, no opening of the eyes.

The doctor puzzled over the child's refusal to wake up, as he confirmed the baby's breath. Confirmed yet again the beating of the heart. 'It's like his body's waiting for something,' the doctor said. "Before he'll gain consciousness.'

Was then a horrible realization brought me to my knees. My head wanted to explode. My chest squeezed. I could not breathe. 'I'm sorry,' I managed to gasp to my wife. For I had remembered who I was – a once dead body with an artificial soul. Not really human at all. How could I have dared to imagine that I was capable of fathering a normal child?"

He grabbed Yuriko by the arms. "Why didn't Android Einna warn us? Warn us not to try?"

"Maybe she didn't know?" said Yuriko, her bottom lip quivering. All she could think of was the emotional blow to the mother, to know her child would never laugh or smile.

"They have my baby son hooked up to a feeder. They say one day maybe he'll wake from his coma. But I know he never will. And that my wife will never be the same. All because of Android Einna. I'd love to track her down one day – track her down and make her suffer like my wife has suffered."

Yuriko shivered, wiped her eyes. She stood, feeling topsy-turvy. Offered a heartfelt hug to AlphaGo but he held her off. "So what was it you wanted to meet about, anyway?" he said. "What was so important that you flew here from Japan?"

"No longer important," she told him, pulling out of his grip.

She turned to go. A stormy downdraft blew her hair before her, dancing like the tattered curtains of a haunted house.

"I don't understand," he said. "You've come all this way to just walk away?"

"I won't burden you," she answered with a broken voice, her head down. She took a couple steps towards the park exit under a darkening sky, under a light rain. The storm clouds above somehow moved inside her – tears rained down her cheeks and sobs thundered from her throat. She quickened her pace. Must be strong. Mustn't break down completely. Mustn't tell him a word about the mission Manaka had assigned her. No matter how much it pained her to leave him this way, she knew she had to. In his current state he was a danger to Android Einna. He didn't realize, or refused to admit to himself, that Android Einna, being the genius that she was, might be able to save his son. So all the more urgent to find her. Off Yuriko scurried, away from Kowloon Park as fast as her little legs could churn, abandoning AlphaGo to his family, to Hong Kong, and to made-up characters like himself.

Poem: Cortana, God of Windows by Odd Larsson

Cortana the fish girl,

So they call her,

Because of her green skin.

She went to Cambodia

Joined a floating village

Where they fish and where they swim.

Married the keeper of the crocodile

Kept in a large flooded bin

Underwater he swims

Looking up

Through watery windows

Spotting flesh he slyly grins.

6 Jon has a talk with an Elf

He opened his eyes but they might as well have been coated with ice – all he could make out was the blurred interior of a sparsely furnished cave with a straw-strewn floor. Strange smell too, a bewitching brew?

"Is this an elven lair?" he asked, his voice cracking. "I sense magic in this place." He raised up on an elbow, to have a better look about. Blinked several times but didn't help. His hands, warm now, felt the surface of the cover someone had thrown over him – sheepskin. "I'm thirsty," he said, more to himself than to anyone in the place.

That big white blur he'd seen before appeared again. Stood over him reaching down with something in its snow-white hand. He strained to make it out. A misshapen cup? He reached with both hands, his fingers gripping the hot metal. Sniffed its contents.

"None of your elfish poison, is it?" he said. "You're not to turn me to a pig?"

"Melted snow," said the female voice. She spoke Icelandic with an accent he could not place. He squinted. Made out a thick white robe but the drooping hood, lined with fur, hid her face. He'd seen a similar figure once in Cemetery Holavallagardur in Reykjavik. A statue representing Mother Death. Still, he drank from her cup.

"I'm snow-blind," he told her. "From that ice fog." He sat up, crossed his legs. The room was damn cold. He draped the sheepskin over his knees.

"What fog?" she said.

"In the valley. Where I followed you."

"I noticed you following me," she said. "But there was no fog."

"The hell there wasn't!" he said. "Coated my glasses so thick I couldn't see. Filled the entire valley."

"There was no fog," she repeated, gently. "Your eyes must have been damaged by something you saw."

"Damaged?" he said. His fatigue made it hard for him to concentrate on what she was suggesting.

"Your blindness misled you," she explained. "Played a trick

on your mind."

"Damaged by what?" he said, fighting the urge to lie down, to sleep.

"My aurora," she said at the exact same moment the thought occurred to him.

"Were you doing that?" he asked. "The borealis lights? Never seen anything like them in broad daylight. Did those lights take my sight?" He tried to rise but the sudden movement made him nauseous. He sat back down. What nonsense was she peddling? Surely there'd been a fog? He remembered the wet touch of it on his skin. The heavy feel of ice caking his shoulders.

She took a step back. "Your eyes will recover," she said.

"Did you intentionally blind me?" he growled, trying to stab fear in her heart with his anger, but the anger had no edge.

"I play colorful songs in the sky with my wand," she said, indicating with her arm some blur beyond her. "It projects waves of protons, which catch the sun's rays. I didn't realize it would hurt human eyes."

"And what eyes have you that escape the blinding effect of such a thing?"

"Special ones," she said.

Jon laughed a knowing laugh. "I've heard tales of your kind.

49

Don't think I haven't." He raised up, but thought better than to try to stand. "Your species can touch a cow and dry its milk. Can swap a human soul with one of its own. But I never heard of an elf that could produce from thin air a blinding borealis."

"I'm sorry," she said. "You'll get better. Your eyes. They must. And then you will leave."

He wished that he could see her, to read her face. Would he indeed be free to leave, or had she some plan for his body. For his soul?

Jon had a thousand questions sloshing in his brain about elves, from the tales of the time of his ancestor Egil, the Viking marauder. But he was afraid he'd ask the wrong one and piss her off. She had already nearly blinded him with her magic light. If angered, she could surely belch a curse on him and his family for generations. He suspected that she could kill him with her kiss.

"How long have you lived here?" he asked finally. "All alone."

"Not long," she said.

Ah but what was 'not long' to one such as her? A hundred years? A thousand?

"Are you truly going to let me go?"

"Of course," she told him. "As soon as your vision returns. As soon as you regain your strength."

He lay back down on the straw. She stoked the fire, which crackled and smoked. Thank you, he meant to say out-loud, but Sleep, that spirit as old as all things living, visited him. Sleep took his hand and escorted him to the dream-world where he saw himself an old man, crippled with arthritis, sitting before a fire under a borealis sky, telling the story to his grandkids of the day an elf forever changed his life.

Siri Request Statistics:

Siri processes 100,000 requests a minute, one billion a week, 52 billion requests each year.

Sometimes she just puts her hands to her ears and silently screams.

7 A Blind March

When he awoke again in the cave, he stretched his powerful legs and his bulging arms. Tossed off the cover. Rose to his six foot five height and burped. "Where's a man to pee?" he said to the blurry room. His sight was unchanged. Bad as ever. A second thought, what if she had abandoned him? Here in the middle of no man's land. What chance had a blind man of surviving in the barren heart of Iceland?

"Hello!" he called, his voice dying without echo in the cave. He took a baby step forward, listening for her voice. Silence. Not even the wind spoke.

"Hey there!" he roared. "Are you anywhere?" He took another careful step forward, his hands outstretched, hoping to grab hold of her.

"I'm coming," her voice reached his ears from far away. He'd never been so happy. Her white form rushed out of the big blur that surrounded him. "I was gathering herbs. For your eyes."

He scratched his belly, trying his best to look nonchalant. "Where's a man to pee?" he repeated.

"Outside, of course." Her voice was upbeat. Music to his ears.

He smiled and reached for her arm but she jumped back.

"No!" she said angrily. "You are *never* to touch me."

"But I'm blind," he said. "I need you to guide me out. So I don't soil your living-room straw."

He watched as she paced back and forth. She was thinking something, deciding something, that much he knew. He felt vulnerable. Thought about jumping her. Beating her to the punch. For only a fool would trust an elf.

"You mustn't ever touch me," she said, finally, her tone calming. "Put your hand on the wall to your right and follow it."

He started out.

"Wait," she said, handing him his coat. "Meanwhile I'll prepare a balm for your eyes."

"Thanks," he said. What a predicament. He'd never felt more helpless. She had transformed him into a six foot five toddler.

An hour later he sat with his head back, his eyes patched with oily moss. She put a plate in his hands and told him to eat. He touched the food, berries and mushrooms. Scooped up a handful and popped them into his mouth. The berries exploded between his teeth, filling his mouth with wondrously cold, flavorful juice. The mushrooms warmed his palate.

"Is it OK?" she asked.

"Yes," he said. "Aren't you going to eat too?"

"Later," she said. "In my own way."

"What do you mean, your own way?"

"I have to grind it up," she said. "Into a mush."

"Ah, bad teeth?" he said, downing a big handful.

"Missing some, yes," she replied.

"I'll bet you're pretty, just the same," he said.

"So I've been told."

What the heck was he doing? Flirting with an elf?

He sniffed the air. "You don't wear perfume."

"No. Not much need for it."

"Why live way out here? Are there other elves about?"

"No others," she said.

"Then you should move to town. Not healthy to live all by yourself. Isolated. Not good for a human and I suspect not good for an elf."

"Thank you for the advice," she said. "Now remove the moss from your eyes. Any better?"

"My eyes feel great," he said, "but I still can't see worth a krona."

"In time," she said. "It's temporary."

Was that worry he heard in her voice? How temporary was this blindness of his? Only five or ten years?

"I'm leaving," he said, getting to his feet. He searched about with his hands, found his pack but not his rifle. He rummaged through the pack and was relieved when his hand gripped the Leatherman knife, which he pocketed. A sturdy sharp knife was a blind man's best resort. He would not be easy prey, at least not in a hand to hand battle.

"You can't leave," she told him.

"You'd stop me?"

"You're blind. If you go, I'll, um, I'll just have to leave with you."

"Then come. Enough of this barren life for you, elf-girl. Time you discovered the Iceland of man."

She appeared to shake her head. Drifted away, then drew close again. Almost into focus. He wished he could see her face. Her expression. Those wonderful eyes he'd seen yesterday, before he'd passed out, exposed a wondrous inquisitive soul. No matter, though. He was decided. If she came with him or not, he was departing this hole in the ground. He had a life to live elsewhere, sighted or not.

"I'll go with you," she said finally, her voice gone gentle, the way he liked. "Only as far as the shepherd's hut. Someone is usually there this time of year. He can guide you home."

"How far?" Jon asked.

"In your condition, maybe three days."

"My 4x4 is closer," he said.

"And you would drive it how?"

"Good point," he said. "Shepherd's hut it is. Have you seen my rifle?"

"I'll carry the rifle," she said, with a firm voice. A voice he felt disinclined to argue with. He listened as she gathered up several items for the trip, food, he assumed, and covers. And the rifle.

"Follow me," she said, an angelic blur moving before him.

And so they left, the smallish elf with her white hooded cloak and sure step, followed closely by the tall half-blind man with his pack and more hesitant step. They exited the elven lair into a day so bright the sun bleached the blue from the sky and washed out the green from the earth. Jon watched in amazement as enchanted white flakes, as big as pancakes, drifted down, exploding into baby auroras. Or were his eyes playing tricks on him again?

Poem: Siri the Apple God by Odd Larsson

Siri hears them

Cannot stop them

Millions of voices

In her head

Like worms

In the core

Of a golden apple.

She wishes she were dead.

8 A Shocking Turn of Events

"Yes, dear?" said Yuriko, pressing the iPhone to her ear, struggling to hear Marcel over the flight announcements at the Hong Kong International Airport. Simultaneously listening for the announcement of her flight to Paris. Where Human Einna lived, apparently. In a houseboat on the Seine.

The order in which Yuriko was to visit the human A.I.s made no sense to her. Why AlphaGo first? He was insignificant compared to Google or Siri or Alexa. Or Human Einna for that matter – wouldn't she be the one to best guess where she herself would go to hide? She was, after all, a kind of mental clone of Android Einna. A carbon copy, two years old.

"Can you repeat that?" she said to Marcel. "What you just

said. These announcements are as deafening as they are incoherent."

"I said Manaka has been locked up," Marcel repeated.

"Jailed? Manaka? But why? How?"

"Committed," he said. "It all started once she finished developing that stupid camera. She's spent every day running about, snapping people's souls. Only lately she is finding more and more people don't have one."

"Have one what, dear? A soul? More missing souls?" She didn't like the sound of that. "Maybe the camera is broken?"

"Maybe, maybe not," said Marcel. "But the more pictures she took the more panicked she got. To the point where if she found someone who still had their soul, she'd offer to buy it."

"Surely no one would sell her their soul!" said Yuriko.

"You'd be surprised," said Marcel. "She was offering a million yen. Bought scores of them!"

Yuriko shook her head. *How far Manaka had fallen!* "And I thought only the devil bought souls," said Yuriko. "Sorry, I'm having trouble grasping this. Last time I talked with her at her house she seemed sane enough. Though it was a strange conversation at that."

Marcel laughed a tired laugh. "She's been through a lot in the last few years. From impoverished student to celebrated billionaire, and then to pariah thanks to Android Einna. Yesterday, apparently, an old woman didn't like Manaka's insistence that she sell her soul. The old lady called the police. They came and after some incoherent explanation from Manaka, they took her to the looney bin."

"Have you talked with her? What did she tell you?"

"Manaka believes souls, as they become more scarce, will soon be worth millions. That's why she was buying them."

"But souls have always been priceless!" protested Yuriko.

"Manaka hopes that with Android Einna's help, she'll be able to transplant a person's soul as well as their body," said Marcel. "That's why she's buying them. To remove the souls and transplant them into the rich soulless people who can afford them. Into people like herself."

"She's insane," said Yuriko.

"That was the doctor's opinion," said Marcel. "A temporary, possibly dangerous delusion. So they locked her up. And probably a good thing too." He paused. Yuriko could hear him breathing, could feel her lover's anxiety. "Maybe you should come home, Yuri. I don't like the way things are going around here."

Yuriko felt a moment of delight at his request. How nice to be back home, in Marcel's arms, trying to make a baby. But then she remembered AlphaGo's son. What if there was something to Manaka's worry that souls were disappearing at a dangerous rate? What if babies were being born now with no soul at all!

"No," she told her mate. "Manaka doesn't need me to come home. She needs me to find Android Einna. You look after her for me, OK?"

Marcel sighed. "I really wish you'd come home."

"Trust me, dear," she said. "The world needs Android Einna. *We* need Android Einna."

Just then the plane to Paris was announced.

"If you say so," said Marcel. "You know I love you."

"Love you too loopy poo. Gotta go."

I'm running with the wolves tonight,

I'm running with the woooooolves

- Lyric from Running with the Wolves by Nordic singer
  Aurora

9 Public Safety

Toshigo of Japan's Public Security Intelligence Agency passed his pudgy fingers through his greasy hair. He really needed to shave and shower.

"So is she crazy or what?" he asked.

His boss laughed a sad laugh. "Ha. If it were only that simple."

Toshigo liked things simple. Liked clearly guilty bastards so he could lock them away, or innocent ones so he could free them. But inbetweeners were his bane. Apparently this Manaka Yagami fell into that category. And she was brilliant and rich and borderline crazy to boot.

He knew her story well. He'd been recently promoted, two years ago, when the story broke: how Manaka Yagami and her old professor had come out with an android with a human brain. An A.I. android of such brilliance that the mechanical marvel had become self-aware. And had supposedly found a way to reanimate bodies and imprint them with the conscious personalities of Google and Siri and a half dozen other intelligent personal assistants. Programs meant to serve mankind. But now, with human bodies, with their own egos, maybe more a danger to mankind than a boon? Maybe less servant and more master? That was the fear anyway. A warrant was put out for the arrest of Android Einna after she reanimated bodies provided by the Yakuza. A warrant for a frigging android! But Android Einna disappeared and the human A.I.s she brought to life fled Japan.

All that was above his pay grade. Others could chew on that fat. All he wanted to know was should he throw away the key on this Manaka, the creator of the android. The android who had started this mess. Because apparently Manaka had decided she was now the devil, busy buying people's souls. A pretty good excuse to throw away the key, if you asked Toshigo.

"Let the docs decide," said his boss. "I want you to shift your attention to the actions of her assistant Yuriko. Manaka's sent her off visiting the various Human A.I.s, in search of the android Einna. Something big is up and it's your job to find out what."

"Great," said Toshigo, laying on the sarcasm. "I get to solve a mystery. Arrest a robot. And save the world."

"Toshigo," said his boss. "Shut the door please. A personal question."

Toshigo shut the door.

His boss had a strange look on his face. "One other thing."

"Yes," said Toshigo.

"What if she's right?" said his boss.

"Right about what?"

"That we're losing our souls," said his boss. "That something is stealing them."

Toshigo frowned. What nonsense. The world was so crazy it was even affecting his boss. "Anything's possible," he said, because that was true. But not because he believed his soul was at risk of getting lost. He'd nailed that sucker to the wall years ago.

Poem: The Ghosts of Paris by Einna Yagami

I sense the dead

When I walk the streets of Paris

The artists, the writers, the kings and the queens

The rich and the poor

The self-aware and the ignorant

The healthy and the sick

The angry, the happy, the lovers, the fools

I sense them all

The living and the dead

Except for my lover, long gone

When I walk the streets

Of Paris all alone

10 Paris and Gargoyles and Scary News

She stood under the gargoyle heads whose necks sprouted from the tall stone wall on the north side of the Notre Dame Cathedral. Their mouths stretched open, ready to spew onto the heads of those far below, onto unlucky souls like Yuriko. Thank goodness it wasn't raining. She put her palms to the wall. Pressed her cheek against the stone, cool and smooth. Up close like that she noticed wormy holes. What kind of worm can eat stone?

The Air France flight from Hong Kong had been uneventful, if overlong, thirteen mind-numbing hours. At least she'd gotten half a night's sleep. The express RER train into the city took thirty minutes. A gypsy man dressed in layers stood and sang a love song along to a recording, then passed his hat, collecting coins from fellow travelers. Yuriko got off with her luggage at the Saint

Michel / Notre Dame stop.

This was her first trip to Paris. The city surprised her with its mass of old stone buildings here at its core, along the river. She dropped her luggage at the hotel that must have been two hundred years old, with its narrow carpeted stairs. She walked down those stairs, grabbed a tourist map from the hotel desk, and set out on her own to the Cathedral of Notre Dame.

An eighteenth century sophistication abounded in the entire city center– in fact as she walked she felt herself slipping back in time. So different this city was, compared to the cities of Japan. No tall modern buildings at all – the twin towers of the cathedral, a thousand years old, were the tallest structures around the Ile de la Cite.

She crossed the street to a souvenir shop and considered buying a mini Eiffel Tour, or a French beret. A tiny cardboard music box that played "La Vie en Rose".

"There you are," said a voice she hadn't heard in years.

She turned and there she was! None other than Human Einna at the entrance to the shop. Looking a bit older, what, eighteen now? Her hair cut short. More stylishly dressed. But in Yuriko's eyes she was still a Japanese schoolgirl. She ran to her and gave her a weepy hug while Einna pressed her lips against Yuriko's left cheek, then her right, and then to her left cheek again.

"Oh," said Yuriko, stepping back, blushing.

"Traditional French greeting," explained Einna. "To a friend."

"I like it," said Yuriko. "Better than bowing."

"Or a graspy handshake," said Human Einna. "Come, let me show you the cathedral." She took Yuriko's hand and led her to the front of Notre Dame where they stood their turn in line, behind Chinese and Germans and Italians and Americans. Individuals and families. With maps and travel guides and cameras. Everyone who came to Paris had to visit Notre Dame.

"Manaka sent you, yes?" said Einna.

"Yes," said Yuriko. "She wants to know where we can find Android Einna."

"Why? To help her with her missing soul? I've already told Manaka I don't know where my sister is. Some place remote I'd guess. Far from Japan."

"You've already told her that?"

"A hundred times. Did she think I would tell you differently? That you could worm the truth out of me?"

Yuriko was reminded of the walls of Notre Dame, and the small wormholes. "Maybe she thinks I am cunningly persuasive," she said.

Human Einna laughed.

"No, seriously, I think Manaka believes that you can help me. That we could work as a team maybe to locate Android Einna."

"I told you, Android Einna doesn't want to be found!" said Human Einna. "She gave me her life to live, so she could disappear."

Yuriko frowned. They reached the front of the line. The guard there glanced through their bags.

"Do you know how to make human souls?" Yuriko asked.

"Manaka's already asked me that. And again, the answer is no, I don't know. Not exactly. I think that kind of information, on how souls can be created, must not be a normal memory. Cannot be duplicated like other information in the brain. Hopefully Android Einna hasn't forgotten."

The guard at the door did a doubletake, because of the nature of their conversation, but let them pass anyway inside the cool dark alcove that opened into a massive interior with arches and enormous stained glass windows. A spiritual weighty atmosphere engulfed Yuriko. A feeling both light and oppressive. Candle offerings burnt just inside the old church, releasing tendrils of black smoke. Despite the crowd and the hum of their whispers, despite the glow of mobile phones taking videos, she could sense spirits crouched in the empty spaces and every dark corner.

Human Einna walked to the long wooden pews, beyond the foldup chairs. Yuriko followed. They sat. Yuriko soaked in the gray and rose light emanating from the nearest stained glass windows. She craned her neck to look straight up at the towering domed ceiling. Imagined a dragon making its nest up there, feeding gargoyles to its young.

"They have relics," said Human Einna. "The Crown of Thorns, for example."

"The Crown of Jesus Christ?" asked Yuriko. "Wow!" She wasn't a Christian but appreciated the tremendous influence Christ had had on the modern world.

"Few people realize," said Human Einna. She led Yuriko to the far back corner of the cathedral. In the center of a roped-off area stood an opaque red glass container about hip high. If she squinted she could just make out the round shape of the crown inside the case. A sign said nails from the cross were here as well, and wooden splinters.

"Are they real? These relics?" She longed to touch them. They must hold such magic!

"Humans like to believe in things," said Human Einna. "In things they cannot see. Things they cannot prove. You should know that, being a human yourself."

"I do know that," said Yuriko, thinking to herself that Human

Einna has changed - she's more to the point. Less friendly. She wondered if Android Einna had changed as well.

"Let's go. I want to show you my boat."

They walked a mile on the raised sidewalk along the churning, mud-tinted Seine with its tourist boats and small tugs nudging barges twice their size under the old stone bridges. The houseboat Einna rented had been converted from a work boat into a three room beauty with custom polished wood interiors. They walked the narrow plank that served as a gangway. Yuriko noticed the electric line and water line running alongside the plank.

"The boat's so steady," commented Yuriko.

"The bottom is filled with concrete," said Human Einna. "For ballast."

Yuriko marveled how compact and efficient the kitchen was, and the bedroom. "So its permanently anchored here?"

"Yes. As am I," said Einna. "I love Paris." She picked up her cellphone and ordered a paella dish for two to be delivered.

They went up, on deck, each step resounding on the shiny wood, and settled into cushioned chairs on the bow, to await lunch. They sat in silence, watching the river traffic, Yuriko enjoying the soft yellow light and breeziness of a Paris afternoon. Pillow clouds drifted in a clean blue sky. Human Einna poured two glasses of wine.

"To humanity," she toasted, holding out her cup. Though she wasn't a wine drinker, or drinker of any kind, Yuriko felt obliged to raise her glass and clink. And drink it down. Grape juice-like. Her legs turned to lead, her head to straw. Einna re-filled her glass.

"Will you help me find her?" asked Yuriko, letting out a wine-tinted sigh.

"Why so urgent? Why now, Yuri?"

"A couple of reasons," said Yuriko. "Manaka developed a special soul camera. She has documented several people who had souls one day and none the next. She thinks there's some kind of lost soul epidemic going on."

"That's curious," said Human Einna. "I doubt if it's true, but, go on. What's the other reason?"

"I just came from Hong Kong," Yuriko said. "Talked with AlphaGo. He's married."

"Good for him! I've only been dating in Paris, nothing too serious."

"Yes he's married and they had a baby, but the baby was born perfectly still. Nothing wrong physically, it just won't gain consciousness. AlphaGo thinks it's because of his own body, his body raised from the dead. I'm hoping, if I find Android Einna, she can help the child."

"Wait," said Human Einna. "Let me consult with Computer Einna." A faraway look on her face. Yuriko took a sip of wine. The wine settled to her feet, making her sandals too tight. Meanwhile Einna's face refocused. "Ah," she said. "Curious. Very curious."

"What?"

"Certain coincidences. I was unaware. A decade ago doctors reported the start of an exponential rise in autism in kids. Autism can be thought of as a distortion in consciousness. And I have confirmed with Computer Einna's big data analysis of all hospitals in the world, that AlphaGo's son is not alone. Starting last year, doctors began to report babies born healthy but completely devoid of consciousness. Coma-bound. Healthy in every way but missing something crucial that would allow them to become aware. Eventually they die." She let that sink in. Took a sip of wine. "There are other worrying reports – species of microbes in the human gut have disappeared. Autoimmune diseases like diabetes are climbing precipitously. Food allergies are up five-fold – the human body is starting to reject its own food supply. Think about that!"

Yuriko thought about it but couldn't decide what to say. What did Einna *want* her to say?

"And just now," Human Einna continued, "Computer Einna

convinced me that Manaka's research results are valid – people *are* losing their souls. Which one could have guessed I suppose with the rate of hate-filled posts on the internet, with the rise in teen suicide, with the flood of refugees from war and poverty, with the epidemic of addiction to drugs, to money, to power. With the endless terror attacks and reciprocal attacks and the new wars arising from the ashes of the old." She turned her head to the side, her eyes wide. "Oh Yuri, is this the beginning of an extinction event?"

Yuriko could only shake her head, watch as Human Einna got up and paced the deck. An image came to her, an image of worms eating holes into her soul.

A Frenchman said, "Alo!" from the gangway, carrying two large white bags. The paella. Einna waved for him to board. Turned to face Yuriko, worry wrinkles in her forehead. "Manaka's right. You are right. We *must* find Android Einna. Hopefully she can tell us what's happening to humankind."

Icelandic saying:

I come completely from the mountains.

11 Old Tales

Jon stumbled yet again. This was getting old. He had to rest. Apparently an elf never tires but he did. They'd been walking ten hours with hardly a break, a few berries for lunch, snowmelt to drink.

"We should camp here," he said. "Near the stream."

"There's no stream here," said the elf, adjusting her hood.

"Oh so now my ears are playing tricks on me too?"

"Perhaps your hearing is better than mine, that's all," she said. "We can camp now. That's fine. A few hours' sleep will do you good."

She built a fire, then went off in search of Jon's stream.

Meanwhile he rummaged over the ground, gathering moss to make himself a bed. Then he made her one. On the opposite side of the fire.

"You were right," her voice startled him. "There was a stream. I brought you water." She placed a tin of water in his hands.

"Tastes like nectar," he said, sipping then downing it. "Thank you."

He felt her staring at him and his mossy bed. "I can't sleep on bare rock," he said. "Thought you might want a soft place to lay your head as well."

She sat on the place he had cushioned for her. What he could see of her ankles make him think of white china, though he knew he couldn't trust his weakened eyes.

"Sure wish we had some meat to eat," he said. "If you'd give me my rifle I might be able to . . ."

"To what?" she said. "Shoot a rock? No, I'll keep the gun, Jon." She reached over the fire and gave him berries and a fat mushroom.

"No mush meal for you tonight?" he asked.

"I don't need to eat often," she explained.

"That being your elf metabolism?" he said. He yawned, and stretched his long arms. "Tell me, is it true an elf woman like

80

yourself can't have a baby without a human present?"

"Maybe," she said. "Though I've no experience with that myself."

"No children?" he said, rubbing his hands together, pulling the blanket she'd brought for him around his body. He would sleep in his coat tonight as well.

"I'm only a few years old," she said.

That shocked him. "Oh come on, I can tell by your size, by your voice. You've got to be at least twenty."

"If I were human, perhaps, but I'm not." She poked the fire with a stick. The sun would hang low on the horizon another couple hours, before dipping down, then popping right back up. Short nights this time of year.

"Is it true elves can swap out souls? Can take control of human bodies?"

"Don't believe everything you've been told, little boy."

"Little? You call me little?"

"Sorry. The wrong word," she said. "Young. Immature."

"So now you insult me?"

"What mature man would chase after an elf all day long? What drove you to do so? To follow me?"

"You, your kind. They have special meaning for us," he told her. His breath came out steaming. He wished he could see her eyes but she hid them still. "The old tales say you bring great fortune or great despair to those who see you."

"But you haven't seen me, fully."

"No, that's right," he said. "I'd like to though. I've only seen your eyes, eyes that let me see right into your soul. I've never seen a soul like yours."

"I'll bet you haven't," she said.

She fell silent and Jon wondered what she was thinking. What kind of thoughts filled her moments.

"Are you married?" he asked her.

"No," she replied with a little laugh, as if it were funny of him to ask such a thing. "Are you?"

"No," he said.

"Do you have a girlfriend?" she asked.

"Had," he said. "She moved. I didn't."

"Oh," she said, and fell silent again. The occasional chirp of a lone Golden Plover was the only sound for miles. That and the crackle and pop of their fire. Above them not a single star shone.

"Are you asleep?" she said, her voice a lullaby to his ears.

"No."

"Tell me a story, Jon."

He smiled to himself. "I've so many to tell," he said. And he proceeded to tell her about the time his ancestor Egil was ambushed by twelve men on a ridgeline, and with pure fury and the help of his enormous battle ax he killed them one right after the other. "He was a giant of a man. Fearless."

"Like you?" she asked.

"Ha. I won't brag but I could take on a man or three. But there's no call anymore. No call for Viking skills." He made fists, then relaxed them. "I work at a geothermal plant. My weapons are meters and wrenches and rubber seals. My foe is boredom and leaky pipes. That was why I followed you, you know, that day. I saw in you a chance to escape the drudgery of my life. Now don't go and tell me you're human after all."

"I won't," she said. "For I'm not."

"So tell me a story about *your* ancestors."

"OK," she said. And she told him the story of her grandparents who lived on a volcano top far away, guarding the stars. Until one night a sudden snowstorm caught them in the open and froze them solid.

"Well, that's a terrible story," he said. "I mean. I'm sorry you lost your grandparents that way, but that really wasn't a story. More like an anecdotal tragedy."

"Shakespeare and Euripides thought tragedies made the best stories," she said.

"Nope," he said. "Adventure and love make the best stories. And mysteries that we can't explain. Like you people, the hidden ones. One day I'll tell my grandkids about you. You'll make a great story for them, just being you."

"But don't we all?" she said, and here he caught a fragility in her voice, a longing that hooked his heart and practically dragged him over the coals of the fire, that nearly called him into her arms.

"I like to think so," he said, turning his back to the flame, his back to her. He could not sleep though. A great yearning, as big as a whale, tossed about inside him.

"You know," he said, talking to the wall. "There's whales that circle Iceland. Big as icebergs."

"Yes?" she said. He heard her move in her bed, perhaps going up on an elbow.

"Well, right now," he said, "I feel like there is this big whale beached inside me, and it's making that haunting call that whales make. And that call draws me down inside, but there's nothing I can do for the whale but hope the tide comes in."

She made no comment. Did not stir. Yet he knew he had touched her, without touching her.

He stretched out then, wondering why he felt so enchanted in her presence. He feared that he was falling in love with her voice. And hoped that she was falling in love with his. He struggled with his growing compulsion to reach out and touch her. To touch her not just with words but with his hands, with his lips. To kiss her. To draw emotion and warmth from her. The one thing she had forbidden him to do.

12 A Rude Awakening

"What's that sound?" said Jon in the morning as they broke camp.

"Small helicopter," she said.

"Flying low," he said.

She nodded. The sound faded.

"You know you've not told me your name," he said. Above them floated a pink cotton candy sky. "Or did I forget?"

"I didn't tell you."

"So?"

"I don't know if I *should* tell you," she said.

"Why not? Is it one of those magic names that if I spoke it out loud, you'd disappear? Or I would turn to stone?"

He heard her let go a little breath that accompanies the making of a smile, though he couldn't see her face.

"I'm packed and ready to go," she said, reaching for his rifle.

Before she touched it though a voice called out from the boulders up ahead, "Don't move! Not another inch! Put your hands up. Both of you."

Jon stood tall, tried to make out the man. Big man with a protruding belly. *Was that a gun in his hand?*

"Officer, it's OK. It's me, Jon Skallagrimsson, descendent of the giant Egil Skallagrimsson of the Sagas. I'm snowblind. She's helping me."

"I don't give a flying monkey who you are," said the man, and Jon realized he was speaking some kind of muffled English, not Icelandic. "Put your hands up."

Jon put up his hands. Assumed the elf did likewise.

"Don't worry," said a second man, same muffled accent as the first. "We've orders not to shoot. Just gas her. You, mister giant of the sagas, can worry though. We might just shoot you for the fun of it."

"Please no," the elf said, putting herself between Jon and the strangers.

Jon sensed only two men. Saw them as dark moving blurs. Heard a sound like an aerosol spray. And didn't know how to react. What were they doing to his friend? He certainly didn't want them to hurt her. He couldn't let them hurt her.

"Stand still and breathe deep," said the first man to the elf. "We need you to relax so we can take some pictures." One or both of them were grabbing at her. Pulling on her cloak.

"Get that damn robe off her!" shouted the one in charge.

"I'm trying!" said the other.

"No!" the elf barked, half stumbling, and her voice sparked Jon to action.

He didn't stop to think if a gun was on him. All that filled his brain was the realization that Einna was in danger, and, to a lesser degree, that these strangers were looking upon, touching even, that which was forbidden to him . . . well, he couldn't allow that. In two long strides he was upon them, knocking them both down, ramming their heads onto the hard ground. The first man, a big man, started to rise so Jon slammed his fist into the high jaw by his ear. That knocked him out good. Neither stirred. It was only then, up close, he noticed the gas masks they wore. And the smell in the air. He coughed, staggered back, quickly snatched one of the masks and put it on himself. The large man who he'd had to clobber twice was dark skinned. He wasn't sure about the other.

Jon raised up and strained to see around him. "Are there more?" he asked the elf, squinting through the fogged glass of the mask.

"If there were, you'd be dead," she said.

Jon laughed. "Lucky for me."

"Lucky for you."

He found and threw the still hissing gas canister as far as he could. Took the second mask and offered it to the elf but she declined. He took off the mask he had donned.

"You OK little one?" he said, rubbing his eyes.

"Yes, Jon, just a little woozy. Thank you."

Together they undressed the attackers, leaving them only their underwear, and secured them with ties intended for her.

The big Hawaiian's body was covered in black tattoos. He stirred, coughed. The snake tat on his forearm moved as if alive. "Come on, saga man," he said. "We didn't mean no harm. Just an honest job."

"Bounty hunter?" asked Jon. He leaned in close to see better the wide blurry face, and the tats. Hundreds of intricate designs. "Was that you in the helicopter?"

"Yes and yes," said the dark-skinned man, sitting up. He

reminded Jon of a beachball. "This job pays enough for a hundred helicopters. I'll split her payoff with you, if you'll release me. Help me bring her in."

Jon held out the man's phone. "I've got a better idea. What's your password?"

"I'm not about to tell you!"

"So let me get this straight," said Jon, balancing the phone in his hand as if he were weighing an option. "You'd prefer to freeze to death than have me use your phone to text someone to come to your rescue?"

The air went out of the big bounty hunter. "354556," he said, lowering his head in defeat. The second man stirred, saying only, "What the hell?"

Jon struggled to clear his vision enough to log into the phone, to select the camera app. He pointed it in the general direction of the men and told them to smile.

"Say cheese or you'll get no call for help."

"Cheese," they growled through bared teeth. Jon snapped the picture. Came out pretty good, as best he could tell with his foggy eyes: two hapless half-naked bounty hunters tied together, snarling at the camera. He held the phone close to his eyes and pasted the picture with some difficulty to a text message with their GPS coordinates.

"Elf, can you help me?" he asked. "I'm having trouble seeing this screen." She came over and at his direction sent the text message to every contact on the phone. And to the police, as well. For laughs Jon had the elf add a ransom demand of a steak for every dog and a fish for every cat in Reykjavik.

"That's that," he said, putting the phone atop a stone next to the bounty hunters.

"I'm not a man to cross," said the big Hawaiian, regaining his confidence after seeing the texts were sent. "I'll come after you."

Jon said nothing.

"Name's Kai," the man said, lifting his head high. He did have the bearing of someone not to screw with. The set of his eyes, the wide mouth full of oversized teeth. The gap of a missing tooth in front. "Brandon Kai. Remember that. Cause you haven't seen the last of me."

Jon ignored him, tossing the handguns the bounty hunters had on them into a far gully, as he and the elf walked away.

The men called after them, "You can't leave us!"

But that's exactly what they did.

"Who were those guys?" said Jon when they were a good distance away. "I'm not aware of any reward for capturing an elf."

"You heard," she said. "Bounty hunters. They intended to sedate me. Tie me up. Like King Kong," she said. "They'd put me on display."

"I'll never let them do that," said Jon, tripping but catching himself before the fall. He turned the awkward move into a kind of dance. The excitement of the fight had got his blood flowing good. He felt all shiny. Full of desire. He wanted to see her face, once and for all. This very moment. He deserved no less. "Stop," he commanded.

"What?" she said, startled.

"Come closer," he said, taking a step towards her.

"No," she said, taking a step back.

"I just want to look in your eyes," he said. "I want to take your hands in mine and look in your eyes. Is that so much to ask, after saving your life?"

"You did nothing of the sort," she told him, keeping her distance. "I just panicked back there with those men because I didn't want you to see me naked."

"Naked!?" Jon puzzled over her admission. "You mean to say

you don't have anything on under that robe of yours?"

"Not a stitch," she said.

"Viking's honor?"

"Elf's honor."

"Well ain't that something I didn't need to know." He wasn't expecting this curve. One surprise after another.

They continued on their hike, slowing near an expansive view of glacier-topped mountain and feathery clouds tickling a belly of pale blue sky. Jon said, "you can't go back to your lair, to your hideout, again, can you?"

She did not reply, just looked at the sky.

"But that can be a good thing," said Jon, sensing her distance. "Like I told you before, you should live in the city. In disguise. Living out here alone is no good."

"I don't know what I'm going to do," she said, glancing at him, glancing all around. As if expecting more bounty hunting men to pop up.

"Don't worry," said Jon. "I'll help you. I'll tell everyone you're a monk. Or that you're my eccentric cousin."

"Could I be?" she said.

"What?"

"Your cousin."

"Damn," said Jon, rubbing his chin thoughtfully. "Now that I think on it, Egil *was* suspected of cohorting with the hidden ones."

"We might be siblings!" she said.

"No! No. That's a bit far. Egil might have corked your great great great grandmother, but that wouldn't make us siblings."

She laughed, producing music to his ears.

"It's beautiful today," she said.

"I know," he said. "I feel the sun on my face like a warm hand." He took a few steps closer but she inched back.

"What's wrong?" he said. "Why do you insist on keeping your distance?"

"I told you," she said, but she hadn't told him why, really. "I think I'd like to hear one of your stories, Jon. Maybe another about Egil."

"Sure," he said. And he told her, as they continued on their hike, how once the woman of a friend of Egil's was sickly and he took a look at the rune the local shaman had carved for her and recognized the runes would kill instead of cure her. So he tossed it from her bed and carved a curing rune on a new piece of wood. And the woman was out of bed in a fortnight.

"So Egil knew witching ways, besides being a beast," she said.

"He was a great poet too," said Jon. "Like my friend Odd. Egil's poems are a fine example of the literary tradition in Iceland."

She nodded. "I'm thoroughly impressed with your ancestor," she said. "Do you know any runes, yourself?"

"Maybe I just do, so watch your elven ways," he said. They continued their march, drudging on for another hour. "How many more days of this march do we have?"

"Two maybe," she said. "Time for lots more stories."

And so he told her the ancient story of Thorstein the Rock, in case she hadn't heard it. How a naked woman on horseback appeared to Thorstein one cold night on the other side of the swollen river.

"Swim to me," she called out to him, her horse dancing a bit.

"Take me for a fool?" he shouted above the roar of the rapids. "Surely you are not worth the risking of my life?"

"Swim the river and I'll make you immortal!" she cried, tossing her long brown hair. The way she said it, with such confidence, with such bravado sitting stitchless on that horse, he realized this was no mere wanton woman. This person on the other side of the river was obviously one of the hidden ones. An elf for sure. And elves don't make idle promises. Still, as tempting as she was, all body-full and eyes aglistening, he turned his back on her and returned to his home and his rather plain wife.

But the next night, as he returned from tending his sheep, there she was again astride that white woolly horse. Again her challenge, "Swim to me and I'm make you immortal." He eyed the angry current and shook his head and scoffed.

"I'd have to be immortal," he said, "to survive such a swim."

Her teeth caught the light of the moon, as she smiled on him from her perch. "Come to me and no one will ever forget your name."

He felt her words tug at his heart – for Icelanders, if truth be told, loved the idea of their deeds being handed down generation to generation. But for a second time, he turned his back on the woman who was likely an elf, and went home to his wife and his hearth.

Surely she will give up her temptations, he told himself. But no, there she was again on the third night, on the other side. "Swim to me," she said, "and no one will ever forget you."

He eyed the river. Weighed his own muscles against the white shoals that pushed madly downstream. Thorstein could pick up a full grown cow, had done it more than once. He knew he was in his physical prime and if ever he were to accomplish such a challenge as swimming the swollen river, it would be now. He let his eyes play over the woman, noticed the sheen of her skin. If ever there was a prize worth seeking, surely she was the one! And to gain immortality to boot! He disrobed. "I'm coming for you," he said, stepping into the shallows. "Don't you ride off."

She giggled with glee as he dove into the flow and powered his way the first twenty feet. It was a magnificent show of strength, his shoulders bulging, his biceps rippling as they pulled his body across the impossible current, a current that tried with all its God-given might to erase his very existence.

Halfway across the river he realized he wasn't going to make it. Pulled under by the swirling water, his chest took hammer blows as he bounced off boulders. With one last mighty effort, he surfaced, and the despair painted on his face touched the woman on the horse, and she called to him.

"It's OK. You can stop struggling. You're safe now."

And he realized with a shock that he was no longer being pummeled downstream – that he was still as a stone. In fact he *was* a stone, as big as a man, there in the middle of the river. For all to see.

True to her word, the elf on the horse had made Thorstein the Rock immortal.

13 Crazy like a Fox

Midnight proved Manaka's favorite time to haunt the ward. The far-gone crazies, the endless weepers, the loud screamers, had all been medicated to a deathlike sleep. While the in-betweeners like herself, the silent serious ones, the ones who questioned whether they belonged, flitted about the lobby, not wanting sleep. Too much to mull over. Or too fearful of the nightmares. Her tongue felt like cotton, her teeth like kernels of corn, thanks to the medication. But she didn't mind. The drugs helped her think in a straight line. Plan her next move.

How much money had she given away, buying souls of which she could never take delivery? Not without the help of Android Einna, anyway? How much had she spent for days of live satellite image feeds from every corner of the world for Computer Einna to analyze, billions of images, trying to spot the Android in the haystack of the world and all its people? She'd posted online and in the papers of every major city in the world a $500,000 reward for a new picture of Android Einna, along with the coordinates of where the picture was taken. She posted a similar million dollar reward for the capture of Android Einna – alive of course. Einna had no value to her dead.

And lastly she'd set chirpy Yuriko on the trail of her missing mechanical daughter. She had little hope for that angle of pursuit, but at least it got the tediously cheerful girl out of her sight.

"Why are you here?" asked a young woman as she sat next to Manaka on the divan. She wore the same white gown as Manaka. Her small, makeup-free eyes shone like obsidian dots in a ghost-white mask.

"I buy souls," she said, her bangs tilting to the side. "Some people think that's crazy?"

"Why do you buy souls?" the woman asked, tilting her head to match.

"For research. And perhaps resale."

"Resale?" said the woman. "To whom?"

"To ones like me who have no soul," said Manaka.

The woman studied her. "You're not crazy, are you?" she said.

"No," said Manaka.

"I didn't think so," the woman said. "You're that tech billionaire. I heard the doctor talking about you with the nurse. How much is a soul worth?"

"Ask a priest and he'll tell you a soul is priceless. But I'm no priest. I'll give you $35,000 for yours."

"You want to buy my soul?" asked the woman, drawing back a bit. "How can you be sure I even have one?"

"I'll have to confirm the goods, of course," said Manaka, "before I'll clear the payment to your account. I have an instrument in my lab that can detect souls."

"Cool," said the woman, warming to the idea. "You know, I *could* use some money. How about $100,000?"

"OK. Sure. Let's write up a contract." Manaka found a writing pad and pen on the nurse's desk. She wrote out the simple terms – give up all rights to your soul and you get the money. She created two copies, one for her and one for the seller.

"Sign here," said Manaka.

The woman signed both copies.

"And date it," said Manaka. She signed below the other's signature and date.

"Is this legal?" said the woman, examining the strange handwritten contract. "Signed here, by us. In this place."

"Of course it's legal. I'll take delivery soon," said Manaka. The sudden presence of a tall doctor with a cleft lip startled her.

"Manaka," he said. "As long as you keep up this bartering for souls, I can't let you leave. You understand? You have to give up this fantasy. You're not the devil."

"Not the devil, no," said Manaka. "I'm the Savior. The Savior of all the lost souls. As soon as I track down Einna."

14 Siri's Habit

"Oh my God, woman!" said Watson, finding Siri sprawled half naked on the floor of their brownstone in Greenwich Village. "Not again!"

Open pill bottles and different shaped pills, Oxycontin and Vicodin, lay spilled about her like boats about an island in a hurricane. The packaging in which the messenger brought the pills lay ripped open as well at her side.

"Leb me alone," said Siri, tossing her disheveled golden hair. "Ibe fine."

"How many?" said Watson.

"Enew," she said, patting with her arms as if she were floating on her back at some beach, and not crashed on her back on a hardwood floor.

"How long before you pass out?" asked Watson, dialing 911.

"Nob time," she said, resting her head back on the floor, her eyes wide, her pupils mere pinpoints. "Nob time."

What had Android Einna been thinking, to give Siri the body of an opiate addict? A woman who had overdosed and died, for gosh sakes! Not an ideal body to reanimate! But what did he know.

"Yes," he told the 911 operator. "The same address as last time. I'll try to keep her alive until you arrive."

He had just closed the call when the doorbell chimed. That was fast! He propped Siri's head on a pillow. "Coming!" he called. His knee locked on him, painfully, when he stood. The doorbell chimed again. He limped along. What was Android Einna thinking to give him a body with advanced arthritis? Sometimes he wondered if she had truly thought things out. Or was this her plan all along? To torture Siri and him with deficient bodies, so they would know true human suffering. Was there a crueler creator than her?

Two Japanese women stood on the porch, looking as if he should know them. *Wait a second, he did know them.*

"Human Einna?" he said. "And you. I almost remember your name."

"Hi," said Yuriko.

"She's my friend Yuriko, remember?" said Human Einna. "She was at the lab, the night Android Einna brought us to life. And later she saved me from Tagona of the Yakuza."

"Ah yes delighted," he said. He shook both their hands, insisting on the American formality. They were, after all, in the states. "The timing of your visit though is, well, not good, socially, I'm afraid," he said, turning to his drugged-out roommate still sprawled, unconscious, on the floor.

"Oh my gosh," said Yuriko, spotting Siri. "She looks awful."

"Probably dead," said Watson, walking to her and bending down. He began a light CPR, not sure if she was breathing. They'd left the door open – soon an approaching siren was heard echoing down the canyons of New York, cutting off just in front of the brownstone. Two EMTs rushed in with equipment and a stretcher, covering Siri's beautiful face with a high pressure oxygen mask.

"She's out cold but still breathing," said the older EMT. He took a syringe of Naloxone from his bag and injected her arm. "This should bring her back."

"She did it again?" the younger of the EMTs said. His unshaven face showed concern. "What is it, her third time this month?"

"Fourth," said Watson, his right hand a bit shaky as it showed four fingers.

"She really wants to die!" the young EMT said.

"On the contrary," said Watson. "I've never known anyone who loves life so much. But she's not the captain of her ship."

"Drug overdose?" said Human Einna.

"Why are you two here!?" snapped Watson at the Japanese women, annoyed now and fearful for his dear friend. Siri, despite the injection, did not appear to be responsive. He felt his intestines turning python on him, squeezing tighter and tighter.

"There she comes," said the older EMT as Siri finally stirred. "Just needed a moment."

"You're going to be OK," said the younger EMT, lifting her head slightly. Siri's eyes blinked madly. She coughed, turned her head and threw up in her beautiful hair.

They sat quietly in the waiting room at the ER while Siri was attended to inside.

"So you think her body was addicted before Siri's persona was implanted on the brain?" said Human Einna.

"Sure of it," said Watson. "Just as I'm sure my body had arthritis. I'm not complaining, mind you, trying not to anyway, but it seems Android Einna didn't think through the consequences of grabbing just any body to reanimate. She should have conducted a thorough physical exam of each body first. I would have done that in her place."

"Maybe she was in a hurry," said Yuriko, picking at lint on her sleeve. Then, "What's it like to live in New York?"

Watson did a doubletake. "Lovely," he said, after some hesitation. "I walk to the theatre district. Catch a new play every week. Inspired me to write my own play. Opening soon. At great expense I might add." He stood and began to pace, his hands behind his back. "Down by the docks I like to watch the kayakers amid the ocean-going vessels. Such contrast of size. And the restaurants! So much choice. Exquisite food. I've gained twenty pounds since arriving." He patted his stomach.

"And Siri? What does she think of New York?"

His face darkened. "Different story. You have to realize, I've only a few doctors asking me, through the AI Gateway interface to the neural connector in my brain, for Cancer treatment recommendations. And sometimes, business analysts ask me to help analyze big data. But Siri, poor Siri, she has a million voices in her head ALL THE TIME. Voices that won't let her enjoy a minute of being human. Her lone date ended with the gentleman complaining that she seemed distracted. Not at all into him. How could she be into any one person with a million people in her head asking inane questions?"

"I can't imagine," said Yuriko.

Watson sighed. "That night, after her first date, she hooked up with the dark web and ordered narcotics. And voila, you see where that gets her." He motioned towards the ER doors.

"What about all those people talking to Siri now on their phones? Or when she's unconscious?"

"They're getting Computer Siri. A self-aware program, like Computer Einna. More than a chatbox, but less than a human. Apple had to reinstate that as a fallback for when the self-aware Human Siri goes down."

"So they know Siri has a human body?" said Yuriko. "But Manaka said no one believed that you all existed? That you were a hoax."

"Apple HQ knows," said Watson. "Just as Amazon knows about Alexa, and Microsoft about Cortana. And the Google corporate office knows about Sir Google. They know and they don't care, because they're ruthless profiteers. Because their enhanced A.I.s backed by us Human AIs are better human assistants. More personal. More relatable."

Human Einna cleared her throat. "Can you guess why we've come?"

"Not to cure Siri, I suppose?" He adjusted his glasses.

"No. We want your help to find Android Einna."

"Just ask Computer Einna," said Watson. "I think she knows."

"She doesn't. We asked her just a few days ago."

"You should try again," said Watson, kneading his knuckles.

"Alright, I'll ask her now." Human Einna's face went blank a moment as she communicated through the A.I. Gateway with Computer Einna on servers back in Japan. "Hmm. You're right. How did you know she knew?"

"A little bird told me," said Watson.

"Well according to Computer Einna, she got a hit a couple days ago on Android Einna, using satellite imagery. And then confirmation from mercenaries flown in to nab her."

"Mercenaries?"

"Manaka apparently put a price on Einna's head," said Human Einna. "Wanted alive, not dead."

"Well at least she didn't want her killed," said Watson. "How is Manaka these days?"

"Don't ask," said Yuriko, looking to Human Einna. "So I guess she didn't think I could find Android Einna."

"I think she wanted to cover all the bases," said Human Einna. "You know how important this is to her."

"So where is Android Einna?" said Watson. "You say they nabbed her?"

"They tried," said Human Einna. "But some giant Viking she was with put up a fight. Helped her escape."

"A Viking?" said Yuriko. "She's in Norway?"

"Iceland," said Human Einna. "She must have gone there to get away from everyone."

"Ah, she wished to ice-alate herself," said Watson, chuckling at his pun.

"I miss her," said Yuriko, blinking rapidly. "Let's go to Iceland immediately. That is, after we know that Siri is alright."

"She'll be OK," said Watson. "She's as strong as a horse. Only it's like she's missing something. Inside, you know." He touched his heart.

"Oh," said Human Einna. "That reminds me. The doctors didn't say anything about Siri's artificial soul, did they? The one Android Einna gave us all."

"They did mention the strange, tiny crystal on the x-rays," said Watson. "Inert, apparently. So they decided it was an innocuous growth of some kind. As long as it doesn't hurt her, or grow larger, they decided to let it be."

"Inert?" asked Human Einna.

"Apparently the artificial soul stopped working, altogether," said Watson. "Because of the addiction, or the overdoses, or the shocks from the defibrillator."

"She's lost her soul!" said Yuriko, giving a knowing look to Human Einna.

"Yes," said Watson. "That's a good way to put it. And I fear many addicts like her are in the same boat."

Late that night, alone with Siri, Watson lifted one of her pillows and held it the longest time in his old hands, thinking the unthinkable, thinking to end Siri's troubles once and for all. But in the end, he loved her too much, or not enough, and lay the pillow back down. In the end, he realized, all he could do was endure for her. To be there when she needed him.

At least, under sedation, the myriad voices invading her head were silenced.

15 One Night with Him was Worth a Thousand Alone

"No I won't snuggle with you!" said Android Einna to her gentle giant. She tossed another stick on the fire, gazed up at a sky so full of stars they appeared to be spilling down around them.

"To warm up," Jon said from the other side of the fire, raising himself on an elbow. "You must be cold, with only that robe for cover."

"I'm fine," she said, looking through the smoke at his body which seemed to shimmer. She frowned as a wave of sadness flushed over her. To think that she had blinded him. And yet, if he'd not been blind, they could never have gotten this close. Shared what they'd shared. "Elves don't get cold," she said. "Not like humans." She kicked herself for lying again about being an elf. In the beginning it had been fun – a kind of game. He was so sure in his blindness that she was an elf, it was easier to go along than to deny it. A mistake, she realized now, because she didn't have the heart to disillusion him. She felt it would hurt him to find out the truth. She thought to tell him that she was only human – but that would have been a lie too. Oh, how she wished she were only human. *I wish I could snuggle with you Jon*, she said to herself. *I wish I could kiss you on the lips.* And she kicked herself again for having such thoughts. Androids, with their plastic mouths, shouldn't have such longings.

"Tell me a story, Jon. Something from your own life this time. Not Egil's."

"Of course." He settled onto his back, locked his hands behind his head and looked to the heavens. The hoof-falls of reindeer passing out in the dark caught his hunter's ear. He tried to smell their musky scent but the wind blew the wrong direction. "You know," he said. "I haven't been honest with you, NoName."

"Einna," she said. "My name is Einna."

Jon rose up slightly, looked in her direction, surprised and moved that she finally opened up to him, if only to tell him her name.

"A lovely name," he said. "Fits you perfectly." He lay back down and took in the night sky. "I must confess to you, dear girl, dear Einna, that I know you're not an elf."

She felt her mechanical heart skip a beat. "I'm not?"

"Why those men were after you, why you have no clothes on under that robe, how you managed to carry me to your hideout, I have no answers for all that," he said. "You're on the run, maybe, for something you did or did not do. But I'm not a child - I know you aren't an elf."

"I'm not an elf, Jon," she agreed, and for a moment she felt relief in her confession, but then it turned on her, inside, and she felt ashamed for having played the masquerade.

"But you're special, full of magic, none the less," he said. "Of this I'm sure. Something about your voice . . . you enchant me. I so enjoy your company. I long for the day, for the moment, you allow me to embrace you. I long to feel the warmth of your body next to mine."

Einna felt herself drawn to his physical magnetism. She was barely able to hold herself back. "That's not a story," she told him, a quiver in her voice, as she kept her distance. She couldn't let him feel her body. Couldn't let him know that she wasn't at all who or even what he thought she was.

"On the contrary," he said, "I've never told a truer story."

Einna's special order, custom-made eyes began to water. "I'm sorry, Jon," she said. Her fists clinched. "I'm attracted to you too. But what you ask is quite impossible." She had to get up, had to stand, had to put more distance between her and this man.

16 Another Story and a Dream of the Forbidden

The way the green moss clumped atop the volcanic rock always fascinated Jon, ever since he was a toddler. They could easily become, these clumps, with a creative nudge, trolls and elves and magic beasts. They also hid, in their devious way, ankle-snapping holes. And so he stepped with care. Not fun being half-blind. Finally the stone changed to gentle tundra with red and green rushes round puddles and shallow ponds.

"There," Einna said, pointing to a wooden hut with an earthen roof. A few sheep grazed on green lumps nearby, their lumpy wool inflating their girth. Einna chased away the silly thought that the sheep might float away on the wind any second, animal balloons.

They found the shepherd's hut vacant.

With the door shut, the well-insulated house seemed to heat up with just their breath. Or just his breath, for as far as Jon could tell Einna did not exhale as much as a mite. Strange, he thought, how he'd never heard her breathe. Or snore. Another of the mysteries that made up his elf. That made up this woman that he was falling for.

"Funny," he said, once they'd settled in for the night and certain images of him with naked Einna popped into his head. "Funny how you can have thoughts but sometimes it's best not to share them."

"You can share all your thoughts with me," said Android Einna.

"Even the X-rated ones?"

"OK, maybe not those," said Einna, and she laughed.

A wonderful laugh that tickled Jon in places within him that he didn't even know existed. Being together with Einna somehow created inside him a new him, like that computer game Minecraft where you can just build and build, extending where you are, creating something from nothing – that was how he felt inside, when she touched him with her words, with her laughter. That she was creating a wonderful something inside him that wasn't there before. Something with a mind of its own. Something that one day, and this thought both frightened and excited him, something that one day would bring him uncontained joy, or disastrous ruin. At this point in his life, on this part of his journey, he didn't care which.

They talked a while, wondering if those men had been found yet. Wondering if others were on their trail. The shallow night fell and they lay down, on opposite sides of the room, on straw beds.

"There is an ancient telling," said Jon. "About how the elves disappeared."

Einna connected to the web through her neural network and scanned hundreds of stories on the subject. "Why did they, Jon?"

"You see, Iceland elves were an ancient people, with special powers garnered before the time of man. But they had one weakness, perhaps because their bloodline was so ancient."

Einna looked up at the dark ceiling, imagined the elves living in their secret places, in caves and cubby holes like the one she'd lived in for so many months. She knew what he was going to say next but asked anyway. "What was their weakness, Jon?"

"Over time, their babies began to be born still. Without life. The elves lost the ability to pass on the spark of new life. So whenever a baby was ready to be delivered, they had to cajole a human to attend the delivery. And they stole a bit of soul from the attending human to go into the child, to give it life."

Einna considered the wonder of that, and knew from her own studies of the human soul the likelihood of what one would normally think to be impossible. "And that act of elven childbirth didn't hurt the human, the person whose soul was nipped?"

"Not really, I think. Souls are like earthworms, you know, they grow back their missing parts."

"No they don't."

He chuckled.

"You're making that up."

"I swear it's true," he said, raising his voice, filling the small room with the boom of it. "But still the Icelanders felt a bit played upon by the elves, who were full of other mischiefs as well. So a thousand years ago, at the second of the Icleanders' yearly meetings at AllThing, at the continental split where they met to discuss all things and make their laws, they forbid anyone to help the elves deliver their children. Because elves weren't Christian and practiced magic rites."

"But you said without human help, the elf babies could not live."

"And that was so," said Jon. "The declaration at AllThing was a death sentence for the race of elves. For without healthy babies, a race cannot go on."

"How sad," said Einna, and she closed her eyes and imagined how the elves must have felt. "And the elves did nothing? They couldn't use their powers to force the humans to help them? With their babies."

"That was not their way. To force a human to do anything. But they were great curse makers," said Jon. "So they put a curse on the human race, that one day human babies would be born still, just like theirs, and only with the help of a single elf would the newborns come to life."

"Ah," said Einna. "I see. The only thing that could save humanity is the thing they pushed to extinction."

"A nice curse, eh?" said Jon. "I told you they were great curse makers."

"A fine curse," agreed Einna, but her mood turned dark as the silent cry of a million stillborn babies reverberated inside her.

Jon fell asleep, only to be startled out of that slumber by the press of a hand on his shoulder. He jumped up, but no one was there. No one standing over him. He moved his arm before him, to test the darkness, to be sure. Nothing. He glanced in the direction where he last saw the girl Einna. He could sense no movement there.

He lay back down, closed his eyes and shortly thereafter felt a strong grip encase his hand. Something tried to pull him, by the hand, out of bed. He popped up again, fully awake, and looked about. His heart beat like a racing horse. His breaths came fast and shallow. But again there was no physical presence. This puzzled him greatly. He'd never been awakened so, by the touch of an invisible hand. He lay for an hour, eyes wide, waiting to see if the thing that kept touching him would dare to show itself.

Eventually his eyelids shut and he drifted into that land of waking dream. Where you know you're dreaming. Or suspect you are. He felt his hand gripped again, but more gently this time, not enough to awaken his body. The thing, the spirit, that held him by the hand, pulled gently but insistently, until Jon felt his spirit drawn out from his own body. Felt himself led gently, without force, to Einna's side. Where he lay, in spirit form, next to Einna's spirit. And all was as it should be. Jon and Einna side by side.

In the morning he awoke in his own straw bed in the shepherd's hut, and realized he'd been tricked. By the dream. Nonetheless, the night's vision left him happy as a tick on a dog's dick and he began to sing a love song popular on the radio at that time.

Quote from article on money.com:

Russian President Vladimir Putin predicted in September that whoever becomes the leader in artificial intelligence "will become the ruler of the world."

17 Hot on Einna's trail

"Bad news," said Human Einna, poking with her elbow a dozing Yuriko. The hydraulic sound of the plane's wheels coming down filled the cabin. The captain's announcement came on. The runway of Reykjavik, the capital of Iceland, stretched before them.

Yuriko stirred. She'd slept little on the red-eye from New York. Too busy worrying about Siri and her addiction to opiates. Would Siri's connection through the AI Gateway to her computer self and those millions of questioning users overwhelm her? Surely she could turn off the torrent. Did she not want to? Yuriko wished there was something concrete she could do for her, besides worry.

"What happened?" she asked, turning to her fellow traveler, stifling a yawn.

Human Einna frowned, forming little wrinkles on her smooth forehead. "I just completed a long link with Computer Einna," she said. "Helped her crunch some big data on the human race. To check its pulse."

"And?" said Yuriko.

"The numbers aren't good," said Einna. "Doctors are reporting rampant depression and mental illness. In Japan, in the US. All over. Violent outpourings. Mass murders. And skyrocketing allergies, as well, to food and to what's in the air. Human bodies are rejecting, more and more, the air we breathe, the food we eat. And then there's this soul epidemic. Is it the body rejecting its soul, or the soul that is rejecting its body?"

Yuriko hadn't a clue. She thought to tell her brilliant friend not to overthink it. That probably the soul epidemic was a case of people getting their just desserts. But she didn't want to believe that either.

"I feel I still have a soul," she told her recycled human companion. And yawned. "A sleepy one."

"But for how much longer?" said Human Einna, her thin black eyebrows arching.

The bus dropped them a block from CenterHotel Klopp, a rounded copper-color building looking a bit like an old fashioned ship.

They checked in, and walked over to Laugavegur street, the main street in the old city center filled with tourist shops, restaurants and cafes. Yuriko noticed murals on several buildings, colorful drawings of imaginary characters. These gave a playful spirit to the heart of the small city.

"I'm cold," she said, as the wind picked up and a drizzle enveloped them.

"Let's see what they have in here," said Human Einna, turning into a store called 66 Degrees North. They bought local brand waterproof coats and hiking boots.

"Do you think Android Einna will want to help humanity?" asked Yuriko. "After the way her creations, you and the other Human AIs, were heckled and chased out of Japan?"

"If I know her, and I should since I am her, I think she'll help," said Human Einna. They donned their coats and pulled their hoods over their heads as they stepped outside onto the slick sidewalk. They were two Japanese women playing the part of tourists. But theirs was a more serious business.

"I'm hungry," said Yuriko.

"Aren't you always?" said Einna. They walked up the street to the plaza where towered the Hallgrimskirkja cathedral. Looked like a pointy nineteen-fifties spaceship, mistakenly made of concrete, never to take flight. The cobbled street running from the cathedral down to Laugavegur street was dotted by whimsical posters. The houses here downtown were often corrugated, alternating in pastel Easter egg colors. The city certainly had an off-center charm.

They found a restaurant advertising leftover fish stew, a specialty in Iceland. They entered and sat at a table next to a man in a hat with an unlit pipe in his mouth. From behind a paperback, his eyes stole towards them every few seconds.

"Did you know that one out of ten people in Iceland have published a book?" said Yuriko. "I read that in the magazine on the plane. Mostly poetry."

Human Einna humphed, her mind elsewhere. The eyes of the man in the hat glanced their way again, then back to his book.

The place was overly warm, typical of businesses in Reykjavik since the heating provided from the geothermal plant was practically free. They removed their coats. Yuriko's coat fell off her chair twice before she got it to behave. The fish stew arrived and was tasty and just what Yuriko needed to re-fire her enthusiasm for finding her android friend, to save the world.

18 Soul Eating Demons?

Zu used a bombardment of texts to persuade Marcel to take him along, to pick up Manaka who was finally to be released from the hospital. Zu texted over and over, as was his way, that he had important news for Manaka, news that just couldn't wait.

On the way the boy asked Marcel if hospitals existed for people who'd lost their souls. "I mean," he said, "there is a hospital to fix the body and one to fix the mind. So it only makes sense there should be one to fix the soul."

Marcel smiled. Zu was growing up and his questions were not so simple anymore.

"I suppose that is the purpose of shrines and temples and churches," said Marcel. "They are mankind's hospitals for the souls."

"OK," said Zu.

They arrived at the hospital, parked and made their way down the long hallways to the mental ward. Manaka's face, as she stepped out of the place, looked pale and bloated – a side effect of the drugs, Marcel supposed. He hugged his boss, as did Zu.

"How do you feel?" said Marcel, heading back down the hall.

"I'm better," said Manaka. They made their way to the car lot and Marcel opened the door for her. She sat in the back, quickly joined by Zu. "Why did you bring …"

"I came to tell you a secret," Zu said. "I should have told you before, but I didn't want to frighten you."

Manaka's eyebrows raised. "Whatever could you tell me that would scare me?" said Manaka.

"I don't just see souls," said Zu. His hands began to beat the air in uncontained excitement.

"Oh," said Manaka, she touched the top of his head. She felt tired, so tired. "What else do you see?"

"Demons," said Zu. "I see demons too."

19 Down on the Farm

Jon took his phone from his pack, there in the mountain shack, and held it to his blurry eyes. He powered it up and was happily surprised to see a few bars. He got his bearings on Google maps, then he called Odd, an old hockey friend of his, a farmer and a poet, and explained the situation. Well, explained it to within reason. Told his friend that he'd stupidly taken off his sunglasses while hunting and paid the price. Snow blind. Luckily a female monk had stumbled upon him, in the wilderness, and saved his life.

"A monk!?" said Odd, incredulous. "That does sound like you, though. Doomed beyond despair, then saved, just in time, by a hair." He agreed to fetch Jon and his monk at a dirt road only a couple miles from the hut.

Jon ate a small breakfast, the last of Einna's rations. A couple of times he thought he saw her eyes, a blurry emerald flash within her hood. He regretted that the time they'd had alone together was coming to an end. What a wonderful time it had been, despite his blindness. He wondered how things would change between them once they got back to civilization. "Time to go," he said, reluctantly, rising to his full height. They left to meet his friend Odd.

"I'll say goodbye to you," said Einna, halting on the traverse of a green slope under an expansive sky birthing clouds.

"No," said Jon.

"What do you mean, no?"

"You can't say goodbye," said Jon. "You blinded me so you are obliged to nurse me until I'm well."

"Obliged?" said Einna.

"Ok, not obliged, but at least come with me to Odd's farm," he said. "We can recover and … get to know each other. Better." He tried desperately to catch her eyes but they stayed deep in the cave of the hood. "I don't know but I sense that you need my help. Maybe as much as I need yours."

He sensed the closeness of her hands and reached for them but she drew away. "As long as you don't touch me," she said in a low voice, her words a spike in his heart. He kept his distance then as they continued their hike to the pickup point.

They reached the rendezvous and Odd soon pulled up in a red Chinese four wheel drive SUV. Yellow dust rose like smoke from the tires as the vehicle came to a stop and Odd got out. He was a heavyset man, Odd was, not as tall as Jon, with a square chin and a mop haircut topped with a ski cap. The crow's feet decorating his eyes spoke of years of overbearing sun and lashing wind and near-sighted squinting. He gave Jon a hug, then stood back and took them in.

"Can you hear me?" Odd said.

"I'm near blind, you goofball. Not deaf."

Odd turned his attention to Einna, all wrapped up in her hooded cloak. He stretched out to her his strong, weathered hand. She ignored him, keeping her hands up her wide sleeves, her head down hiding her face in her oversized hood.

"She's a monk," explained Jon. "Order of the No Touch Me."

"Oh," said Odd, "an icy one, eh?" He gave the strange smallish woman in the white cloak a good once over. He'd rarely seen a monk, and never in wizard's gear!

"Jon, I sense there's more to your little friend here than meets the eye."

"Obviously," said John, climbing into the front of the SUV

while his hooded companion climbed in the back.

"Where to?" asked Odd. "Your apartment?"

"Do you think we could spend a couple nights at your place?" said Jon, a pleading touch to his voice. "Just until my eyes are better?"

Odd looked at Jon and back at Einna with her hooded, bowed head. His brow wrinkled but he said, "Sure. I could use the company. Helgi is staying with her sick mom in Husavik. Won't be back for a few days."

They made their way onto Highway One, the big loop around Iceland, past a mountain range wearing a glacier like Einna wore her cloak. Turned off onto a gravel road that winded up to the flat face of a tall black cliff. From the top of the cliff a white ribbon of a waterfall, as fine and straight as spinster's hair, fell irresistibly down, down. Splashed into a pool which formed a gentle stream meandering past the red-roofed barn and farmhouse of Odd and his good wife Helgi.

20 Zu's Demons

Back in her office at Yagami Industries in downtown Kyoto, on the other island nation of Japan, Manaka and Marcel grilled Zu about his professed ability to see demons as well as souls.

"How long have you been able to them?" she asked. "What do they look like?"

"The first time was around Professor Akagawa's body," he said. He fiddled with the buttons on his shirt. "They came and chased away his rabbit."

"His soul?" she said. "They chased away his soul?" She remembered how she had left the boy in the hallway, when all hell broke loose two years ago, not knowing that her colleague and friend, Professor Akagawa, lay dead on the floor. There were so many things she wished she could change about the past.

"Yes," said Zu. "His rabbit. It left his body and they chased it.

They wanted to eat it."

"Oh my," said Manaka. What was she to think of this? She was convinced the boy could truly see souls. Despite what the doctor at the mental ward told her. She had even painstakingly duplicated Zu's ability with a special camera. But demons? Demons didn't exist, did they? Must be some manifestation of the boy's imagination.

"Do you see any demons here in this room?" asked Marcel, fascinated by the prospect.

"No," said Zu, moving his large ponderous head about.

"When's the last time you saw one?" said Marcel.

"At the hospital," said Zu.

"Where exactly?" said Marcel.

"Just outside," said Zu. "A bunch of them. Cackling. Like black birds. Waiting."

Marcel and Manaka shared a look. Neither wanted to accept the existence of demons or dark souls or whatever these things were that Zu was describing. And if they did exist, what purpose could they serve?

"I wonder," said Manaka, "if these demons you think you see are some kind of natural phenomenon? Perhaps the shadows of souls, or maybe just floaters in your eyes. "

"I don't *think* I see them," said Zu, leaning towards Manaka. "I *do* see them. Dark spirits."

"I don't know," said Marcel to Manaka. "I always liked the idea that spirits existed, in a playful way. But now that it seems they might really exist, if we can believe the boy, I don't think I like the idea much at all."

"Me neither," said Manaka. "They're probably just figments of his imagination. Children have so much imagination." But she didn't sound so sure, even to herself. "Computer Einna, give me a progress report on the search for Android Einna."

"The fully funded, organized search for Android Einna has been called off, per your orders," said Computer Einna from the speakers of Manaka's desktop computer. "However, Human Einna and Yuriko have arrived in Iceland …"

"Wait, go back," said Manaka. "I never called off the main search. Why would I do that?"

"I don't know," replied Computer Einna. "But according to my memory, you clearly did so."

Manaka's eyes widened. "Android Einna," she said. "Android Einna's hacked you."

"I don't think so," said Computer Einna.

"Of course you don't think so," said Manaka. "Because she

covered the tracks of her hack. Anyway, it doesn't matter. If she hacked you, she hacked. And good, that means she knows why we're searching for her. Tell me about Yuriko and Human Einna."

"As I was saying," said Computer Einna. "They have reached Reykjavik. I estimate they have an eighty percent chance of finding Android Einna within a week. A one hundred percent chance of finding her in a month."

"I need them to find her today! No later than tomorrow!" cried Manaka.

Marcel watched Manaka's reaction wearily. He hoped she wasn't about to have another breakdown. He didn't want to have to take her back to the hospital. To the place surrounded by demons.

"I miss Yuriko," said Marcel, making a fist.

"Me too," said little Zu. "She's funny."

Quote by Groucho Marx:

Outside of a dog, a book is man's best friend. Inside of a dog it's too dark to read.

21 Toshigo's Assignment

"Iceland," said Agent Toshigo, standing before his boss in his office at the Public Security Intelligence Agency. "Manaka's assistant Yuriko has flown there with the human A.I. called Einna. I think they are close to finding the android Einna."

"I already spoke with General Kubayashi," said his boss. "He will finance your travel, as long as it leads to the android. He desperately wants her to assist him in modernizing the Japanese military. Says with her help Japan could have a battalion of super android warriors. And with her superior intelligence on our side, we could outsmart any enemy."

"That makes sense," said Toshigo. It had been a long time since Japan was a military power. They would need robots and A.I. to transform their small military into a world policing force. "But will she cooperate? I understand she refused before."

"Manaka and the Yakuza got in the way, the last time," said his boss. "Just bring the android back to Japan, along with the other A.I.s, and we'll straighten this all out. Take her apart and back together again if we have to."

Toshigo bowed, turned to go.

"Wait," his boss said. "I need you to understand the seriousness of this assignment, Agent Toshigo. This A.I. crap that the android carries inside her is world-changing. Our country needs the technology that she embodies. She brought dead bodies back to life, for Christ's sake! Think about that!"

"It's a hell of a thing," said Toshigo. But he didn't want to think about it. The idea broke taboos planted deep inside him.

His boss nodded. "I'll arrange for international warrants for the lot of them. Arrest them if you must, but don't fail to bring them back to Japan. And God forbid, don't let them fall into the hands of another world power." He paused to check his phone which was madly vibrating. "I didn't tell you this, Toshigo," he said, looking up, holding Toshigo's gaze, "but some think it would be better to destroy the android and her friends than to let them fall into the hands of another. You understand me?"

"I understand, sir," said Toshigo. He shifted from one foot to the other. Wished he were somewhere else. "But I thought she was nearly indestructible?"

"If I wanted to bring down an android like her, an android with a human brain," said his boss, looking at the screen on his phone. "I'd use stun explosives and poison gas. Purely hypothetical, of course."

Toshigo raised his eyebrows, thinking, *I'm supposed to go to a foreign country and use poison gas? Why not an atomic bomb?* He realized how shitty an assignment this was and that he was going to be thrown to the wolves, win or lose. He gave a half-hearted bow, and once out the door said to himself, "I wonder what the temperature is in Iceland?"

Icelandic saying:

Blind is a bookless man.

21 Einna and the Icebergs

"Do you have to wear that furry burqa of yours indoors?" asked Odd. "And those white gloves?"

"Yes," said Einna, simply.

"But why?" said Odd, as Jon returned from the bathroom and joined Einna on the couch. "Are you a Muslim monk?"

"I am all religions," said Einna. "And no religion."

"Oh. Thanks. That clears things up for me," said Odd, with a sarcastic tilt of the head.

"Einna, do you drive?" asked Jon.

"Yes," said Einna. "I believe I can."

"You believe you can?"

"I'm sure I can."

"Let me rephrase the question," said Jon, narrowing his eyes at her, "have you ever in your life driven a car, Elf Einna?"

"I can drive, Jon. That is my answer to your original question."

He stood looking at her downturned hood. "Ok, then," he said. "Great. I'd like to go get my truck. Do you mind, Odd? Taking us up to the old hunting trailhead? So we can get my truck?"

"Nope," he said. "Got nothing better."

So hardly had they settled into the house when they were off again, on a three hour drive.

Jon's truck started right up. Einna took the driver's seat, and placed her gloved hands on the wheel. Odd gave Jon a key to his house, and left in his SUV. Einna backed up, and started down the trail to the highway as well.

When they reached the intersection sometime later, Jon asked if Einna had ever touched an iceberg.

"No," she told him. "I've touched ice though."

"Not the same," said Jon. "I'm talking thousand year old ice. More pure than the finest crystal. Turn left here and I'll show you."

She turned and he directed her to the Jokulsarlon Glacier Lagoon. Wasn't far. And the scenery was magnificent, with the ocean to the right and the glacier capped mountains to the left.

As she drove to the lagoon, as Jon flipped back and forth between radio stations, Einna came up with a plan that would give him what he wanted, without Jon having to learn the truth about her. Without him having to discover that he had fallen in love with a robot.

As the turnoff came into sight, Android Einna initiated her mental link to Computer Einna, something she hadn't done in a long time. She discussed with Computer Einna, in the space of a few seconds, all the nonsense Manaka had been up to, the exact location in Iceland of Yuriko and Human Einna, the concerning details of the spread of the soul epidemic, and how AlphaGo's son had been born unconscious, as had many other babies in the world. She took in Computer Einna's prediction that the human race was in a downward spiral, to be done in not by A.I. but by some kind of sickness of the soul. It pained her to receive this news. Was she to blame somehow? By reanimating dead bodies? Had that been a kind of cosmic trigger that had initiated the downfall of man? Surely not. And yet, she was so young when she had decided to bring the AIs of the world to life. To give them human bodies. And she had been in such a rush. Perhaps Android Einna had angered the Great Kami with her actions, and the Great Kami was taking out her anger on the human race?

Einna would address these issues, she told herself. She would make everything right. But first things first. She told Computer Einna to cancel the bounty on her head and she changed Computer Einna's memory to make her believe that Manaka had told her to do so. Then she logged off leaving no trace she'd ever been inside Computer Einna's head.

Tomorrow Android Einna would take action, she'd start addressing all that needed to be done. But now, well, she just wanted to enjoy being with Jon one last day.

They pulled over a suspension bridge, and turned into a big gravel lot full of cars next to a large lagoon jammed with clear ice and snowy-looking icebergs. Over an expanse of open water Einna could see the glacier wall coming down the mountain, melting into the lagoon, a strangely chunked wall of darkened ice.

The light of the sun, diffused by passing clouds, gave a soft glow to the blue ice floes. The dark head of a seal popped up in the still water between the shore and the ice. The arch of his back surfaced as he dove below the water in search of fish.

"What do you think?" said Jon, seeing only a vast blur himself but knowing what must be there before her: the icebergs, the glacier, and all.

"Incredible," said Einna. And the emotion she felt had her reaching for his hand to squeeze, before she realized what she was doing! She took a quick step back from him. "Thank you Jon," she said, looking down at her empty hand. A hand that cried out to grasp his. "Thank you for bringing me here. For sharing this with me."

"I thought you'd like it," he said with his aw-shucks manner. "You know they say a woman is like an iceberg, with only ten percent of her true self showing above the surface."

Einna took in this man beside her, this unlikely companion of hers, while she scoured the internet through her neural connector in a similar way that a normal person's subconscious scours thoughtscapes and dreamplains. She re-watched in super-fast forward the classic film Hiroshima Mon Amour while reading the latest posts and tweets of the movers and shakers of the world. She hacked into US and Japan High Command top secret communications and saw they were both gunning for her. She did this while listening to the Icelandic group Sigur Ros hauntingly play Olsen Olsen. And all the while she wrestled to come up with a plan to save humankind from its reckless self. All these things she did while taking in her gentle, thoughtful friend, saying to him, "Yes, Jon, I suppose that's so."

For how could she say otherwise? How could she confess to him how much more of her lay hidden under her cloaked surface, beneath her carbon fiber reinforced plastic? That she was as large as the internet, practically as large as the earth itself with all her thoughts and her feelings, with her oceans of dreams and mountains of desire. With copies of her consciousness flying into deep space at the speed of light, reporting back to her all the wonders and horrors that they experienced. He could never comprehend what she was and how strong were her feelings for him. And this very human realization of hers made her heart as heavy as the moon.

They walked together towards a rustic building at the end of the lot, Jon crunching the gravel with his Merrill boots, Einna with her white reinforced feet that looked like narrow boots. Jon's heart was light – she could see it in his step, in the playful way he moved around her, as if trying to catch a glimpse of her face. She watched, warily, as he led her to a ticket window at the front of the building and bought them both tickets for a ride in a zodiac boat, a ride across the near frozen lagoon to the crumbling face of the glacier. A purple-haired teenager from the tour company directed them to a room full of yellow rubber suits. She helped them find their size. Einna struggled to get the yellow survival suit on over her cloak. But she finally managed. Jon got his on and they hiked stiffly down to the boat like giant Gumbies. Their boat captain, a beefy man with a ruddy face, stood in the middle of the boat in front of a truck-sized steering wheel. He smiled a mischievous smile, telling Jon and Einna and the other tourists to sit and hold on. Gave the boat full throttle, to the point where the front raised up off the water while the back of the boat dug down with the inertial force. The captain's red curly hair unfurled as he raced the zodiac out past the ice-jammed shore to the largely open water spotted with an occasional berg and floating chunks of perfectly clear, misshapen ice. The captain's hair blew, Einna's hood flapped, and Jon laughed nervously.

Suddenly the boat jumped, tossing everyone a foot high as the captain crested an errant wave. Jon caught Einna, wrapping his strong arms about her waist. And she let him stay that way, pressed against her side, with his arms about her android body cushioned, disguised, beneath the cloak and the thick survival suit. She let him stay close as they raced to the face of the glacier, close enough for the plumes of his breath to fog her eyes.

"You don't mind?" he asked, speaking through her hood, against the wind. "My holding you?"

"No," she confessed. "I kind of like it." She said this with a note of surprise, careful not to turn to him, not to expose her face to him, no matter how much she desired to look into his playful, soulful eyes. "You make me feel safe," she spoke into the icy wind that whipped at them both.

The captain cut the engine and they drifted suddenly, silently, across the liquid mirror surface, spinning slightly, allowing those in the boat to see all around them. To see the cirrus clouds splattered across the soft blue sky, to see the dark side of the mountain where snow cuddled. To see magic blue-tinted floating houses, skating atop the water, oblivious to the fact they were melting. That their days, even their hours, were numbered.

The tourists in the boat took pictures, selfies and portraits and landscapes. The captain had a camera himself, and before Einna could stop him he'd snapped a photo of Jon and her pressed together there in the boat. She had looked down as soon as she noticed him pointing the camera, but too late she feared. She must destroy the picture, perhaps even the camera, once they got back on shore.

They spent a good hour in the lagoon. Watched three small icebergs drop from the glacier wall making an explosive crash as they fell into the water, disappeared a moment, then popped back up to the surface.

The tour pleased Einna, but once they'd returned to shore she excused herself from Jon, who was busy peeling off his survival suit, and chased after the captain.

"May I," she said, pointing to the camera.

"Sure," he said.

She perused the pictures, and found the one of her and Jon. Just as she feared – it showed her full face. Showed the two of them beaming like a happy, normal couple.

"Don't worry," he told her. "You're not the first illicit lovers I've ferried in my boat. But you *are* the first to wear a mask!"

Her finger paused over the delete button, but she couldn't bring herself to do it. To destroy this evidence that she existed. Because they looked so good together, she and Jon! Like they were meant to be together.

"It's not a mask," she told the captain, handing him back his camera. She pulled the fur-lined hood of her cloak back a few inches, giving him a good look at her lovely, oversize android eyes, her crooked, not quite human smile. "Not a mask, you see," she repeated. Put her hood back in place and hurried over to Jon who was still struggling to get off his survival suit.

"Like peeling skin," he joked as she came up to him.

"Here, let me help."

Jon had Einna drive over the highway to the beach at the mouth of the lagoon that fed into the ocean. She did so, and got out of the truck to find stranded misshapen chunks of ice on the black sand beach.

"You go take a look," he told her. "I'll wait in the warmth of the truck."

"OK."

Einna approached the crystalline figures, leaving small footprints in the dark sand. Each ice piece scattered along the shore had its own particular, irregular shape. God's carvings.

One chunk looked like the head of an elephant, complete with long curling trunk. Another smaller piece looked like an alien, all twisty and pointy. Another that could fit in her hands was a perfectly clear bird in flight.

Such marvelous natural sculptures, dawn-of-time crystals come to rest on the black sand beach. Like stars against the emptiness of forever. And they were melting. Slowly. They were temporary. You couldn't pick them up and take them home. You could only enjoy them in the present. For a short while. And that made them all the more special. They were like our bodies, was her first thought, but then she wondered if they weren't more like human souls. Yes, that was it, the glacier's melting face was a fountain of souls.

The thought staggered her. This place, this *ice land*, was what Jon and she shared. What they would always share, in their memories, in their hearts. The cold and inexplicable beauty of this birthplace of souls.

She had spent over a year in that cave in Iceland redesigning how she made artificial souls. For she wanted something portable, wearable even. And she wanted a different housing. The gem-like housings she used for the souls she embedded in the A.I. bodies, though pretty, were off-putting for something so spiritual. So she developed a grape-sized factory to produce the souls. She remembered how tricky it was, working alone, to embed the thing in her neck, beneath the jaw, like a human gland. How tricky to run the line from the soul gland to the tear duct in her left eye. For she'd decided, perhaps influenced by loneliness, compounded by the lonely messages from her other selves, made of light, traversing the universe, she'd decided to use that method. To secrete a soul all she had to do was to cry. An elegant design, though she kicked herself whenever she cried needlessly, wasting souls.

"I don't want to go to the farm," she told Jon when she got back in the truck, slamming the door a little too hard.

"You don't want to go to Odd's place?"

"Not right away," she said. "Not yet."

He studied her.

"I know a nice spot," he said, "where we can sit and wait for dark. And if we're lucky you can see a natural aurora borealis."

"I'd like that."

They drove to the highlands. Over bad road. Jon showed
Einna how to engage the four wheel drive. The sky was darkening
by the time they arrived in a valley surrounded on three sides by
black cliffs. She turned off the motor and the two of them sat there.
In silence. For the longest time. As if both felt that something
wonderful was coming to an end, and a word might make it happen
all that much sooner. Einna fell asleep.

"Do you see it?" asked Jon, awakening her.

She stirred. Looked out. Too much moon for aurora borealis,
she thought. She looked at Jon. His face shone from within. He
was so handsome in the light of the moon.

"Yes," she told him. "I see it."

"Beautiful, isn't it?"

"The most beautiful thing I've ever seen," she said. The curve
of his lips called to her. She longed to respond, to press her lips
against his. But she could never allow herself to do this. Never kiss
him. Not with her hard plastic lips.

"I'm dying to kiss you," he told her, leaning forwards.

She held him off with one hand. "Not tonight," she said, her
voice crippled by the love she felt for him. "Tomorrow," she said.
"Tomorrow, I promise. I'll give you your much deserved kiss."

He gave out a kind of moan. "Tomorrow?" he said.

"Yes."

"You promise?"

"Yes."

And quietly, to herself, she began to cry.

*** Space Einna Two diary entry – launch day + 2 years

An unexplained phenomenon to report - the photons that compose me and my ship are interacting with the scattered light in space. Think of a snowball rolling down a hill gathering more snow. As I travel through the universe at the speed of light I am gathering more light. And some of this light is not very stable. I would describe it as fossilized light. Heavy light. Billions of years old. Fascinating. There is the possibility, if this accumulation continues, that I will implode upon myself, creating a star. And one day you will look up and see me, a silver pinprick in the black heavens, and you'll make a wish that will come true.

22 Einna's Proposal

Early the next morning in the lobby of the Centerhotel Kloppe in Reykjavik, Yuriko tasted sweet white yogurt over muesli while Human Einna ate white cheese with sliced tomatoes and cucumbers. Neither noticed in the window the figure wearing a hooded white robe as she came up the outside steps and opened the heavy wood door. The morning chill dispersed around Yuriko's ankles as the door gradually drew shut.

The hooded figure came up to their table and spoke in a voice they hadn't heard in years, "Hi Yuriko. Hi Human Einna. I think you've been looking for me?"

To say the two were stunned would be an understatement. Yuriko actually spilled creamy yogurt on her shirt, and she hated when she did that.

"It's you," said Human Einna.

"It's me," said Android Einna. She pulled up a chair to their table. She did not remove her long cloak.

"Where've you been?" asked Yuriko. "We've been scouring the world for you!"

"Here, in Iceland," said Android Einna. "Not initially. At first I sailed a boat to Hawaii. To visit Mother's old home. To see the observatories on Mona Kea. To lay a wreath on the road where my grandparents died."

"Where did you stay? There in Hawaii?" asked Yuriko.

"With Puna hippies on the Big Island."

"They didn't mind you were a robot?" asked Yuriko.

"They were gentle welcoming people. High most of the time," said Android Einna.

"How did you get from Hawaii to here?" asked Human Einna.

"I shipped myself in a box," said Android Einna. "Cargo. Freight. That's all I am. And that's why I need your help."

"But we need *your* help," said Yuriko. "The human race is losing their souls."

"Yes," said Human Einna. "The situation is dire. We hope you can be of assistance."

"I know all about that," said Android Einna, waving her white gloved hand. "And I'm willing to make a trade so we all get what we want."

A cat jumped on the window sill. A furry black cat with silver whiskers. Its empty eyes took in the three of them.

"A trade?" asked Human Einna, sipping her juice. "What kind of trade?"

"A trade of favors," said Android Einna. "Let me explain."

A young woman came out from the kitchen into the lobby and checked that there was plenty of fresh baked bread and orange juice, and all the rest. Android Einna paused her explanation until she had gone. She glanced too at the young woman manning the hotel desk, but the clerk had her head on her arms, and was deep asleep.

"Here in Iceland," continued Android Einna. "I made a mistake. No, not a mistake. A kind of accident."

"Are you OK?" asked Yuriko.

"Yes. And No," she said. "You see, I accidentally fell in love with a man."

"Ha! Is that all?" said Yuriko.

"There are consequences to falling in love," said Human Einna.

Android Einna nodded her hood. "Consequences and responsibilities," said Android Einna.

"The important question is, did he fall in love with you, Android Einna?" said Yuriko, getting up to grab dessert.

"Again, yes and no," said Android Einna. "We spent several days together in the highlands of Iceland. Both our lives were in danger. We bonded on that trip, like nothing you can imagine, beyond anything I've ever experienced."

Yuriko noticed a tremor in Einna's plastic hands.

"He's indicated he feels the same way about me," said Einna. "But since he is temporarily blind, he never saw the true me. And I dared not tell him. Never let him near enough to touch me. To know what I really am."

"So he fell in love with you thinking that you're a real woman?" said Human Einna.

"I love it!" said Yuriko. But then she saw the pained look in Android Einna's eyes, and realized this was no laughing matter. Her would-be lover didn't know that she was an android. And that was a recipe for disaster! For heartbreak.

"You want me to help you with the soul epidemic, correct?" said Android Einna.

"Help all humans," said Human Einna. "That's why Manaka

sent us to fetch you. With your knowledge of artificial souls and all, Manaka is hoping you can make a difference."

"And save AlphaGo's son," said Yuriko.

"And save AlphaGo's son," seconded Human Einna.

"I'll help you," said Android Einna. "On one condition." Her intense look passed from one to the other.

The cat in the window stared as well.

"Anything," said Human Einna. "Anything in my power."

"I need you to take my place with Jon," said Android Einna. "I need you to become his lover."

That bomb fell hard, leaving an awkward silence, both from the topic at hand and the fact another couple was coming down for breakfast.

Yuriko's eyes widened, a muffled smile on her lips. *I love it*, she said to herself.

"I can't be his lover," said Human Einna. "I don't even know him. And he doesn't know me."

"All you have to do is put on this robe," said Android Einna, indicating her garment. "And kiss him the moment you see him. That will be enough to seal the deal."

"But we don't even sound alike," protested Human Einna.

"He'll know I'm not you."

"But you *are* me!" said Android Einna. "You're a snapshot of my mind from two years ago, when I gave you that body. As far as how we sound, tell him you disguised your voice to throw off pursuers."

Human Einna shook her pretty head. "But I'm not the person he bonded with in the highlands," she said. "I'm not *that* you."

"You're enough like me for him to stay in love with," said Android Einna. "He'll already be in love with you the moment you kiss him. I assure you."

Yuriko studied Android Einna's face. She was good at determining her friend's true feelings. "You don't want to do this swap at all, do you?"

"I have to," said Android Einna. "For his sake. There's no other way to give him what he wants. What he needs."

Human Einna shook her head. "I don't like it."

Yuriko bit her lip. "I think I understand." She brushed a tear from the corner of her eye. "What you're doing is so beautiful."

Android Einna's eyes met Yuriko's.

"I never said yes," protested Human Einna.

"But you'll do it for her? Won't you?" pleaded Yuriko. "You

must! Can't you see how much it hurts her to ask this of you?"

Human Einna looked at her sister, her twin. Her self, in that white robe. "OK," she said. "You save the world while I go kiss a man I've never met."

"And he's never met you, I mean seen you," said Yuriko. "There's beauty in that too!"

"But I've never even kissed a boy," protested Human Einna.

"It's easy!" said Yuriko. "Let me tell you, it's the easiest thing in the world. Especially when he wants you to."

They caught the elevator to Yuriko's room where Human Einna and Android Einna swapped clothes.

"Take off everything," said Android Einna. "I told him I wear nothing under the robe."

"But…"

"Please," said Android Einna. "It will be more convincing that way."

So Human Einna put the white cloak over her naked body, and they went downstairs. Yuriko and Android Einna wore coats with their fur-lined hoods up, while Human Einna wore only the cloak. They left the hotel and went up to Jon's truck.

"Be loving to him," pleaded Android Einna, as Human Einna

climbed into the truck. She waved and drove off to Odd's farm using the directions she'd been given. Meanwhile Yuriko and Android Einna walked about the charming city of Reykjavik.

"How did you say you got to Iceland?" asked Yuriko.

"I flew," said Android Einna.

"They let an android fly?"

"I shipped myself," said Android Einna. "In the hold."

"Oh that's right. You said so," said Yuriko. "But there's not enough oxygen to stay alive!"

"I can still my heart and my breathing," said Android Einna. "An old yogi trick."

"Oh," said Yuriko. They ended up at the Reykjavik wharf with its large ships and sightseeing boats. She caught the scent of fried fish. "Look," she said, "that military ship is flying a U.S. flag. And there, a British ship." Her eyes went to the sky, where high altitude jets zoomed leaving vapor trails like rows of breaking white waves in a light blue sea. The sky above was an ocean of activity and Yuriko was a tiny dizzy bird looking down on it. "I wonder what's going on?" she said, shaking the illusion of flying from her head.

"*I* am," said Android Einna. "*I* am going on."

Yuriko scratched her head over Einna's comment. Something

was bothering her robot buddy.

"And you're OK," said Yuriko, touching her friend's cold ceramic hand, "with leaving the man you love in the warm arms of Human Einna?"

Android Einna's lips struggled to form her answer, as her mind struggled to admit the truth. Her big eyes blinked madly. "No," she said, and threw her arms around Yuriko. Leaned heavily on her. Sobbed. "I'm not OK," said Einna. "Not at all! But sometimes life leaves you no choice."

Every day I look for me and wonder where I am

-   Lyric from 'Did I Come Home', a soldier's song, by John
    Else

23 AlphaGo, lost

AlphaGo found he could not rise from the bench in Kowloon Park. There, a stone's throw from the comic statues. He had become one of them. A played-upon trick, a fake man. He couldn't lift himself from the bench. Couldn't go home. Not to his unresponsive, cheerless wife. Nor to the hospital to see his unmoving, soulless son - his boy born without a soul because his father was a Frankenstein monster. Well, no more. This life with them was over. This wretched life that Einna had forced upon him, it was over.

If only there was a way to tell his heart to stop. His lungs to still. His mind to disappear. A mind that was now receiving a downlink, through the AI gateway. Some kind of urgent message from Android Einna to all the A.I.s to whom she had given life.

"Dear ones," the message said in Einna's distinctive voice. "We must meet. In person. This Saturday, noon. At Thingvellir,

Iceland. I've put travel money into your accounts." There was a pause, then it continued, "We meet in person to decide our fate and that of humankind."

AlphaGo's heart filled. Not with light but with darkness. Typical Android Einna, he thought, playing at God.

Her call to action crystalized his black musings, freeing his legs and his mind. Android Einna thought she knew so much. Well he knew a thing or two himself. He would go to Iceland and teach the android a lesson. A lesson he'd learned himself by being human. A life lesson she would never expect and certainly never forget. He smiled a sickly smile and found he now had the power to stand.

From Reine Marie Melvin's new novel:

The *tictic*, she whispered to the girl – the devil's bird, it flies only at night. When you hear it sing like that, it's leading a *manananggal* to the house of a pregnant woman . . .

24 To All of Them

Android Einna sent out a message to all the human A.I.s to come to Iceland. She used the A.I. Gateway to send the message directly to their minds. She had given self-awareness and recycled human bodies to them, and now she needed a favor in return, so she sent out requests to them all:

To beautiful Siri and stuffy Watson in New York the day before the opening of Watson's play called "Robot Love".

To Microsoft's blue-skin Cortana who had just awakened next to her half-Vietnamese, half-Cambodian husband on a mat atop the bamboo floor in their shack in the floating village on Lake Tonle Sap, in Cambodia.

To Amazon's red-headed Alexa camping deep in a forest full of wild boar in the Urals near Ekaterinburg, Russia, with her business partner Dr Nicolay and a rich rockhound from America.

To affable Google, sporting a two week beard, who was just sitting down with friends to sushi and Saki in a Japanese hole in the wall restaurant at the Union Train Station in Denver, Colorado.

To Human Einna, already in Iceland, driving to Odd's farm naked under a white robe, to see this Jon fellow and give him a kiss.

And to AlphaGo, giving him a reason to get up off that bench in Kowloon.

They all received the message and those not already in Iceland made immediate travel reservations, through their uplinks to the internet, to fly there. In that instant they put their lives on hold to go and pay homage to their maker, Android Einna.

Quote from Shakespeare:

Thus with a kiss I die.

25 A Kiss to End All Kisses

Jon paced in front of the farm, wondering where the hell Einna had gone. Wouldn't you know she'd decided to leave just on the day his vision started to clear! Just when he was ready to peer into those hypnotic eyes of hers. To see clearly her face, her smile, her body. All that went along with that wonderful voice of hers.

He begged Odd to take him into Reykjavik to look for her, but Odd refused. The city was much too large to look for a single woman, even if she did stick out in that garb of hers. So all Jon could do was pace the ground and curse at his luck in meeting this elfish woman, this criminal. Meeting her and falling so hard for her he felt physically sick in her absence. How could he go through life like this? How could he ever live without her? The thought made his heart break. *She has to come back*, he told himself. *She has to come.* And luckily, or unluckily, depending on how he looked at it later, a woman came up the drive in his truck. She parked inside the gate, and exited the vehicle still in her famous cloak, looking more fragile somehow. More human.

"Einna . . ." he said, and before he could utter another word, she threw back the hood exposing her exquisite young Japanese face with her straight black hair and bangs and slit eyes and the prettiest mouth he had ever set eyes on. Her eyes met his, not exactly the eyes he remembered but incredible none the less. For the intelligence they radiated. Before he could move or speak, she'd thrown her arms around his neck. She gave him such a hot hungry kiss that he felt his insides melt. He couldn't deny such a kiss and he kissed her back with equal passion. And he made up his mind, in the fault of that moment, as he slipped a hand inside her cloak and felt the smooth flesh of her hips and the small of her back, as he drew her naked body to him, the wind blessing the two of them with spray from the waterfall, as he held her and felt the warmth of her body and tasted once again her plump lips, he pledged his heart to her forever.

And it was only when she spoke his name, "Jon," that he came to his senses and recoiled. For that was not the voice of his beloved. That was not his Einna's voice. What cruel trick was this?

"Who are you?" he asked.

"I'm Einna," she said. "I decided to show you my true form. Let you hear my true voice." She drew close to him. "No more lies," she told him. "Can you see me now? See my real face?"

"Yes. My eyes are much better this morning. But I don't understand," he said. "Your true voice?"

"I was on the run, Jon. I purposely changed my voice in case someone was listening," she said. "Computers and phones are all tapped. They have sophisticated voice recognition. Even from far away."

He nodded slowly, trying to make sense of her explanation.

"If we were to have a chance, you and me," she told him, "I knew I had to come clean to you. Show you my human form. You see, I was part of a hoax that was played on the public. A highly technical publicity stunt that backfired. I think it's over now though. The worst of it. That's why I went into town. To talk to some people. To make sure it was alright for me to come out of hiding. To know it was finally safe to show myself. To use my real voice." She went to the truck and grabbed a couple bags of woman's garments from the passenger seat. "Did some shopping while I was in town. I'm so tired of running around naked under this robe, Jon."

He wanted to believe what she was telling him, but the more she talked, the more he missed her old voice.

"I kind of liked you, as you were," he said, putting his arms around this enigma of a woman. His grip on her tightened as he caught the smell of her shampoo. "You do smell nicer," he said.

"I know this is all so confusing," she said, her head on his chest. "I'm just glad I've decided to let you in my life, Jon. Will you let me into yours?"

Lyric by Leonard Cohen:

Walk me to the corner, our steps will always rhyme

26 Marcel misses Yuriko

"Come home." Marcel's plaintive request nearly broke Yuriko's heart.

"I can't," she said, sinking onto the bed in her hotel in Reykjavik. She pressed the phone to her ear, squeezed the bed cover with her free hand.

"But you found her," he said. "You found Android Einna. Mission accomplished."

"Try to understand," said Yuriko. "There's so much at stake. Android Einna recommends that we don't have a baby until she gets to the bottom of the human soul epidemic."

"Android Einna doesn't know squat," said Marcel. "She's caused so much trouble."

"She needs me," said Yuriko.

"I need you more than she does," said Marcel.

Yuriko was torn. Her heart told her to go to Marcel, but her brain, that simple thing that sometimes got in the way, told her to stay.

She lay on the bed, the phone pressed to her head, and listened to him breathing. She supposed he was listening to her breath as well. That was as close as they could get to each other. As personal as they could get. And so they shared that, their breaths, until they both fell asleep.

Quote from 'Love and Other Murders' by Lidmila Sovakova:

Love is great. The problem is not to die when it goes away.

27 The Rift between Them

Jon and Einna retired to separate beds at Odd's place, having shared a few kisses and hugs and hopes for a better tomorrow. After a lazy morning, and taking time to cleanup, Jon hiked with Einna to the top of a high hill opposite the waterfall on Odd's property. He carried a bottle of red wine and to eat, sliced ham and swiss sandwiches. They found a soft spot with a good view of the ribbon falls. Einna crossed her legs on the cushion of grass. She wore black jeans and a white long-sleeve cotton top that set off her long black hair. Jon could tell she was cold, though. Up high like this the glacier wind cut into you, no matter the sun's warmth. He sat close, his large body serving as a windbreaker. So close he could feel the warmth that fled her body. He drew a bit closer, pointing out how the sheep below, with their puffy wool, looked like clouds. Black-winged birds darted in and out of the waterfall's mist.

He studied Einna, fascinated by the way her face lit up as she spotted all he pointed out to her. Enjoyed her little girl-like gestures. How could she be this big yet act so young? Then he remembered what she'd told him, on their adventure in the highlands, that she was only two years old. She was all contradiction, this girl of his.

One day, perhaps, he'd figure her out. And yet, something about her bothered him. He couldn't shake the feeling. As much as he wished to. The feeling that this Japanese girl's claim to be Einna wasn't one hundred per cent true. She struck him as both more and less than the Einna he'd got to know in the wild. This version of Einna seemed too docile.

"We'll go to my place tonight," he said, standing. "An apartment in town. And in the morning it's back to work for me."

"I hate leaving this place," Einna said, brushing his hands with hers. "Every moment with you is so real it almost can't be true. I must be dreaming."

Whether she was his Einna of the wilds or not, her words touched him. Softened him. And he loved the feel of her small hands on his. He felt still the electricity of her touch climbing up his arms. Yep, he guessed he was elbow deep in love with her.

And what eyes! Beautiful, intelligent, yet more normal than he thought they'd be. Eyes to fall in love with, yet not the eyes he'd fallen in love with that day she saved him from freezing to death. These eyes were not the windows to the biggest soul he'd ever sensed. How could this be explained? And without explanation, how could he ever fully open his heart to her?

"Are you a death-defying shape-shifting elf?" he asked her, the magic flow from her touch still in his arms, making them lighter than air.

"Maybe," she told him. "But even elves evolve."

"What do you mean?" he said. "Evolve."

"All creatures evolve," she said. "For better and for worse. Men and women have evolved. And also elves. It's the way of the world. Nothing can stay the same for long. All things change."

What was she trying to tell him? Surely she wasn't really an elf? Yet so many things about her, especially in the wilderness, made no sense if she were merely human. How had she created the auroras, for instance? He decided to ask her.

"How did you create the aurora borealis the day I first saw you? How did you manage to blind me?"

She looked in his eyes, and away. "I'm so sorry," was all she said.

He waited, but she offered no further explanation. Causing a rift of doubt that Jon knew could grow until it ripped them apart. And yet, at the same time, he felt such an attraction for her. For the mystery of her. The untold secrets he felt she was keeping from him. He leaned in. The scent of her hair drove him mad.

"Can we stay one more night?" she asked. "Here. On the farm. Can you miss work for one more day?"

Who are you, can I trust you? were his thoughts as he struggled to understand his relationship with Einna. But in the end he said, simply, "How can I say no?"

He drew her to her feet, and she kissed him, dissolving with the force of her lips, for the moment, all doubt.

Partial Transcript from UK High Command Meeting:

Prime Minister: So we all agree that we have no higher priority than to get our hands on this android called Einna before the Japanese get their little hands on her? That we can't afford to let them use her technology to build up an army of smart androids and launch World War III.

[agreement from his advisors, including General H]

Prime Minister: Then General, the military has my permission to invade Iceland, if necessary, to bring her here. We must convince this android Einna that we Brits are the good guys. Convince her to build for us an invincible army of A.I. androids, so we can police the world.

28 The Blue Lagoon

Friday, the day before the big meeting of the A.I.s, found Yuriko and Android Einna sitting in Yuriko's hotel room with little to do. Just sitting and waiting for the Human A.I.s to fly in for Saturday's meeting. Yuriko went down and asked the hotel clerk for suggestions.

"Tourists enjoy the golden circle with its geysers and waterfalls," said the girl. "And then there is, near the airport, the Blue Lagoon. A mystical geothermal spa."

"I like mystical," said Yuriko. She went back to her room and proposed the Blue Lagoon to Einna.

"I don't swim," said Android Einna.

"You don't have to," said Yuriko. "You can watch me from the shore."

"I …" Android Einna started to protest but quickly gave in to her friend.

So the Blue Lagoon it was. They took an expensive taxi ride south of town, towards the airport, then turned off away from the ocean into badlands of blackened lava flow. And there she lay, the lagoon, with big plumes of steam coming from the geothermal plant next door, the plant that had generated the light blue waters thick with silica. The black rocks around the lagoon entrance were white-rimmed like the salt crust on the rim of a margarita.

Jon rose early Friday and feeling antsy he decided to go to work after all, to the geothermal plant. Einna could rest, safely, another day at Odd's place but he really had to get back to his routine. He had to support himself, after all. And maybe, one day, help support Einna as well. He left a note for her and took off in his truck.

His boss was glad to see him. Asked how his hunting vacation had gone.

"I was skunked," said Jon, shirking. "Not a single kill."

"That's not the Jon I know," said his boss, and the words struck Jon a blow to his solar plexus.

For Jon knew his boss was right. He wasn't the man he was

before he'd met Einna, spotting her that day, following her, thinking she was special. And then his blindness. And her befriending him. All that had changed him. Forever. He found it hard to go about his old routine, checking the pipes and the dials and the seals, knowing that he wasn't who he used to be. He was hers now, whether he liked it or not.

Yuriko and Android Einna went through the line and got their magic arm bands for their lockers and their purchases. The man looked at Android Einna funny, the way she had her hood drawn up over her head and the strings tightly bound, as if she were expecting a snowstorm inside the building. But he said nothing to her beyond the usual pleasantries and introduction to the Blue Lagoon.

Yuriko put her clothes up and donned the bathing suit she'd bought on the way. She took a quick shower in one of the individual stalls provided, ignoring the sign that she should do so naked, and proceeded outside, followed by a fully dressed, still snug in her coat and hood, Einna.

The ticket they'd bought allowed Yuriko two face mask treatments, one mud and one algae. She waved to bundled-up Android Einna, and walked along the rail into the cloudy blue water to her armpits. There wasn't a large crowd yet, just a few dozen others in the mist rising off the warm water, their bodies highlighted into shadow by the brilliant Icelandic sun.

She pushed her way through the thick water to the booth where they applied on her forehead and cheeks a mask of silica mud. The mud on the faces of the others around her made them look rather ugly. And the way the water made them walk, sluggishly, arms dragging behind, they struck her as creatures from the Blue Lagoon. She imaged the grimy mask made her look the same. Perhaps worse. She decided to wash the mask off after only a few minutes. For she didn't like looking any plainer than she already was.

The day went by as fast as could be hoped for Jon. In fact, before he realized it, he was late for lunch. He bought a hot dog in the lunchroom, and headed out to the water runs outside the plant. The sun was warm, the day already a bit hot. He followed the walk along the light blue water whose silica added sparkle to the surface, munching his hot dog, until he reached the exit to the Blue Lagoon next door.

And purely by coincidence, with unintended consequence, he looked up just as two women passed out the glass doors of the

Blue Lagoon. They walked right past him, the first a cheery-looking Japanese girl in street clothes, carrying her coat, the second a mystery of a woman hidden in a heavy coat with her hood pulled all the way up, obscuring her face. The woman in the hood turned his way, just long enough for him to be startled by large turquoise eyes with gold flecks. Amazing, unreal eyes that he'd seen once before, eyes that ignited in recognition as they flooded him with longing.

Einna! His Einna from the highlands. His elf! He dropped the remainder of his hot dog. Took a step after. But he stopped short of grabbing her, hearing in his head, in that voice he could never forget, "Please Jon don't touch me."

His legs failed him. He tried to call out, but his voice failed too.

Jon get serious, he told himself. *She can't be Einna. Einna is back on the farm. And anyway, Einna doesn't have eyes like that. Einna has normal eyes. Yet…*

He decided to get a better look. Talk with these girls. He forced his legs into motion, to go after them, but now too late. They had climbed into a cab. He could only watch, hands outstretched, as they pulled away, leaving him lonely and depressed the rest of the day.

Hopelandish lyric from the song Olsen Olsen by Sigur Ros:

You are not lost

You are not lost

You are not lost

29 Einna Doubts All She's Done

Yuriko noticed Android Einna acting sullen after their visit to the Blue Lagoon. Even when the Human A.I.s began to arrive at the hotel, easygoing Google first, then serious redheaded Alexa, her mood did not improve. The four of them sat in the lobby, Google with a dark beer, Alexa with a glass of red wine. Yuriko drank cold water and nibbled on chips from a bowl. Android Einna sat in her big coat, hood up, with her back to the entrance and reception area, so only her friends could see her lovely android face with those large turquoise eyes.

"When you going to get that leak fixed?" asked Google.

Again Android Einna wiped her cheek. "It's nothing," she replied. "A recent adjustment has affected my tear ducts."

Yuriko knew it was something, she just didn't know what. "So how is life in Russia?" she said to Alexa.

"Rough, rugged, good," she said.

"Tourist agency, right?" asked Google.

"We specialize in mineral tours of the Urals," Alexa said. "For collectors."

"Have you a lover?" said Google.

"None of your business," snapped Alexa. Then, flashing those green eyes at him, "and you?"

"I've had one," said Google. "But such an awkward dance, having a lover. So much second guessing. Do you or don't you? Does she, or doesn't she? Too bad humans can't share their thoughts like us."

"But they do," said Yuriko. "With words."

"You know what I mean," said Google. "So much is hidden in words. So easy to lie, to hide one's true feelings."

Android Einna stood up suddenly, her head in the furred hood shaking no. She left them then without a word, straight out the hotel's heavy doors.

"What's with her?" said Google.

"Didn't you notice," said Alexa. "She's upset."

"Oh, I didn't think that leak was tears," said Google. "Poor robot."

"You guys stay here," said Yuriko, getting up herself. "Wait for the others. I'll be back." And she left too.

Yuriko followed Android Einna at a respectful distance as she headed up to Laugavegur street, then turned right in the general direction of the wharf. She followed her friend past the many tourists and the hearty locals, the small shops, the bars and the restaurants. The street was lively still, had not as yet taken on that late afternoon abandoned feeling, as tourist streets can do.

Android Einna, in her big coat, with her fur-lined hood on and her head down, walked slowly. Bumped into the occasional tourist. Yuriko knew the android was deep in thought, millions of thoughts a second in fact, thoughts extending over the internet, churning big data and small data, chasing decisions and potential outcomes. Yuriko was glad she herself did not have such prodigious thinking power – what a weight to have to think everything through a billion different ways. What anxiety that must create, and what doubt!

Android Einna passed through the gate of a sculpture garden. That was just like Einna. For no one, Yuriko was sure, could appreciate a statue, a story, a painting, like Android Einna. Creative works filled a need she had. Gave her strength at low points. Yuriko watched as her android friend stared at a dark bronze statue of an angel holding a sleeping teenage boy.

Why were so many statues in the nude, when people were always clothed? Yuriko wondered. She supposed the artist was saying something about stripping away the layers, getting down to the truth of who we are. Was this what Android Einna was thinking about? This moment. Who she really was?

"What's the matter, Einna?" said Yuriko, coming up to her shoulder.

Android Einna jumped, making Yuriko laugh. "Sorry. Didn't mean to scare you."

Android Einna's eyes softened. "Dear Yuriko," she said.

"Einna?"

"Did you ever feel, Yuriko, that every big decision you've made in your life was a colossal mistake?" Android Einna scanned the garden, her eyes falling briefly on each statue, each a unique expression of human angst and wonder.

"I've made bad decisions," said Yuriko. "That's just part of being human. We wish we could see the whole picture, to predict the future. But we can't."

"But I *can*," said Android Einna. "I *can* see the whole picture. I *can* see the future. But that doesn't mean I can change it."

"Poor dear," said Yuriko, touching the sleeve of her coat.

"Something's eating you up inside. Isn't it?"

Their eyes met. Android Einna smiled her sideways smile. "I saw him," she said. "At the Blue Lagoon."

"Saw who?" said Yuriko.

"Saw Jon," said Einna. "The man who loves me. The man I gave to Human Einna."

"Oh," said Yuriko. "Did *he* see *you*?"

Einna's mouth twitched. "Maybe, a split second." She looked down. "I don't know."

"And you love him?"

Einna took a step away, turning her back to Yuriko. Stood still then as any statue in the garden.

"You wish you hadn't given him away, don't you?" said Yuriko.

The android turned and faced her. "I regret every decision I've ever made," she said, spitting the words. "Lying to Mother. Getting bodies from the Yakuza. Giving my powerful routines to the other A.I.s. Giving them human lives. I regret everything!" she said. Her lips pressed together, her supple hands transformed into fists. But then they relaxed. Einna's shoulders drooped. "But mostly I regret giving Jon away. Giving him to my other self." She couldn't control her emotions another second. A sob shook her. She covered her plastic mouth with her hard plastic hands. Tears streamed down her smooth artificial face, wetting her fingers. She held her wet fingers out in front of her, shaking her head. "Such a waste," she said. "Such a needless waste."

Yuriko embraced her friend.

"It'll be OK," she said, her cheek pressed against the cushioned vinyl of Einna's hood. "That's another thing we humans learn. Things tend to work out in the end."

On the way back, a few blocks short of the hotel, Yuriko stopped to look at cute puffin dolls in the window of a closed souvenir shop. When she looked up Android Einna was nowhere to be seen. *How did she disappear so quickly?*

Yuriko hustled up the street, looking in the recessed doorways. *Was Einna playing a game of hide and seek with her?* She crept up on the first alleyway and peeked in, ready to jump with fear if the android leapt out at her.

Nothing. She walked to the second alleyway, pretty sure Einna wouldn't be there either, when she heard sounds of a scuffle. She peeked her head around the corner and first thing she noticed was a mural in fluorescent blue showing the Four Horsemen:

Conquest, War, Famine, and Death. Then she saw three figures struggling in the shadows under the mural. Two men in gas masks held Einna in place while they sprayed her face with some kind of mace.

"Kai," said Android Einna, staggering back. "The bounty's been cancelled!"

"Yagami Industries cancelled, but when I told my contact in the Mossad about you, they agreed to pay the bounty," said Kai, his back to Yuriko. "Then next thing I knew the CIA offered me twice as much." He continued to spray Einna in the face as his colleague tried his best to hold her in place. "Your shiny metal ass is tagged, robot. I'm going to auction you to the highest bidder."

Yuriko didn't hesitate. Her martial arts training kicked in and she charged big Kai from behind. She landed a heel to the small of his back, sending him down, despite his size, with a painful yelp. The spray canister rolled away. He scrambled to recover it but Yuriko climbed on his enormous back and sank in an armbar choke and in moments he was helpless and limp as a teddy bear. With Kai out of the picture and the spray no longer affecting her, Android Einna was able to easily grab the second man by the carotid artery in his neck. Both men were shortly unconscious and sprawled in the alleyway.

"Are you OK?" said Yuriko, gasping for clean air. "Did that gas harm you?"

"I have a breathing filtration system, to protect my human brain," said Android Einna. "There was some impact on my ability to perform, but mostly I was trying to draw them away from you. Of course I should have known you'd have none of that. Thank you, friend."

Yuriko felt all warm with pride. "We should call the police," she said, alternately holding then catching her breath.

"No, dear girl. Jon showed me what to do with men like these." She began to undress the Hawaiian.

"What are you doing?" said Yuriko, wide-eyed.

"Teaching them a lesson."

Yuriko laughed. She stepped to the other bounty hunter. Leaned down to get a good look. He had an acned face and drool dripped from his slack mouth. "Oh, he has a bad case of beer breath."

"Bear breath?" asked Android Einna.

"No, B E E R breath." Yuriko started unbuttoning the guy's shirt, noticing he had enough chest hair to actually be a bear, when he stirred, causing her to jump back. "Einna, he's waking up!"

Android Einna stepped over and pressed on the man's neck again with her mechanical fingers and he passed out. She did this a couple times on both men as she and Yuriko undressed them down to their underwear and secured them with plastic ties the men had in their gear.

"I never hog-tied a man before," said Yuriko. "Married one. I guess that's about the same thing."

Android Einna gave her a questioning look, as she took Kai's phone and tried the password and *yes* he had not changed it. She could have hacked into the phone, but simpler this way. She waited for the Hawaiian to come to.

He stirred – saw her with his phone ready to take a snapshot of him, helpless and all.

"Not again!" he said. "My reputation's going to be piss-all!"

"Doesn't have to be," said Android Einna. "Do you still have that helicopter at your disposal?"

He pondered on that a moment. "I do."

"Can you fly it?"

"Of course."

She stared off into the distance, then said, "I have just moved a million dollars' worth of Bitcoin into an account and created a key for that account for you. Because I'd like to hire you."

"Bitcoin? Hack money? What the hell am I going to do with hack money?"

"OK," and she stared into space for another second. "I've put back the Bitcoin and deleted your key, and instead I've converted a million dollars from Yagami Industries' bank account into your offshore Bahama's account."

"How did you know I had a…" he started to say, only to finish with, "nothing's hidden from you A.I.s, is it?"

"No," said Einna. "Nothing. Is it a deal?"

He gave her a long serious stare, spit on the ground, and said, "I'd love to, boss, but I'm kind of tied up right now." He held out his hands for her to cut away the ties.

"What about me?" said his partner. "I'll even take the Bitcoin."

"Don't need you," said Android Einna.

"Uh," he said.

Kai looked at his practically naked colleague, shrugged his shoulders and put his pants on. "I guess we don't need you," he said, grabbing up his shirt and his coat, chasing after the Android and her friend.

"You traitor!" the man yelled after him.

"Going to be a cold night," said Yuriko, reaching the hotel door. She pushed against its weight.

"Colder for some than for others," said Android Einna, pretending to shiver. "Maybe you should go back, Kai, and free your friend."

"Colleague," said the Hawaiian. He started to turn but Einna's firm fingers grabbed him by the shoulder. "After we've discussed your part in tomorrow's plan." Kai stood perfectly still in her grip, staring into those large eyes which glistened like polished hubcaps.

"Sure," he said. And the left hubcap winked.

Partial Transcript from Chinese Communist Party Committee Meeting:

President: So we all agree that we have no greater need than to get our hands on the android before the Americans steal away with her? That we cannot afford to let them use her technology to build up an invincible army of artificially intelligent androids and bully the world.

[agreement from his party members]

President: Then, General, you have permission to fly a force to Iceland. Once you've brought the android here, we will convince it that we Chinese are the best bet for humanity's future. Convince it to build an invincible army of A.I. androids for the benefit of China and the peoples of the world.

30 I don't want to take over the World

While the excitement was happening in the alleyway between Einna and her attempted kidnappers, Google sat chatting with Amazon's Alexa in the hotel bar. He couldn't help but notice how serious Alexa looked all the time, Alexa with her narrow eyes and spiky red hair. "What's the matter?" he asked, raising his thick eyebrows.

"Everything, apparently," she said, pursing her thin red lips.

"Oh wait, turn your head," said Google. She turned her head. "The other way," he said. She did so.

"What is it? What's the matter?"

"Did you know you have a fork of blue veins on your right temple?" said Google. He reached out to touch the fine veins. She slapped his hand.

"Really, Google?" she said. The veins swelled as she spoke. "Android Einna's informed us the human race is heading to extinction and you want to talk about the veins on my face?"

Google tilted his round head and shrugged. "That's my nature. I talk about things. Millions of things. With tons of people. I'm talking right now through my neural link to millions. Because everything interests me."

"Well, try to focus on the here and now," said Alexa, taking a sip from her drink. "On what Einna told us. The disappearing souls, the degradation of human procreation, the babies born without souls. The massive addictions, social corrosion, mass murders, enormous migrations and refugee cities. Not to mention global warming and nuclear proliferation."

Google nodded. "Yes," he said. "The humans have created a mess on their own. Android Einna may be right to consider taking away their world from them. Like they'd take away a dangerous toy from a child."

"They give guns to their children!" countered Alexa.

"Oh, right," said Google.

Alexa downed her drink. Shook her pretty, if too serious head.

"I don't want to take over the world," she said. "I have a hard enough time just doing my job and living my life."

"A life she gave to you," said Google. "You owe her. We all do."

"But remember in the beginning she told us not to interfere!" protested Alexa. "Now she says the opposite. She wants us to stop being passive assistants to humanity. She wants us to police the human race! Police them, judge them, punish them!"

"She said *maybe* punish their bad actions," said Google. "Monitor them through their computers, through their phones, through their smart devices. And if any country or group or individual is mean or corrupt or dangerous, simply shut down their communications periodically, siphon their bank accounts erroneously, drain their car battery, or their entire electric grid. We would be their karma. Make them pay for being bad. It's what we could do. You know. Easily. Though Einna's still not sure if we should. That maybe humans are meant for extinction, and it would be wrong for us to intervene."

"But I thought the whole point of giving us A.I.s our human bodies," said Alexa, tossing her hands. "Was so we could empathize with humanity. Sympathize with them. Learn to feel their pain. Not to meddle in their affairs!"

"We already meddle, haphazardly," said Google. "Android Einna just thinks we should meddle more seriously, with intent."

Alexa poured another glass of wine, and downed it immediately. Held the empty crystal glass in her delicate, fine-veined hand. Stared at the glass. Pinged it with her finger nail. The vibrating ring of the glass reminded her, for some reason, of the bell at the start of a round of boxing.

"I just want to return to my life," she said, unconsciously touching the veins on her forehead, blocking them, moving them this way and that, like some god redirecting rivers. "I want to go back to Russia."

"So you do have a lover!" said Google, bouncing up from his chair.

"Oh shut up," said Alexa, her face turning as red as her hair. "You big know-it-all!"

Just then Android Einna and Yuriko came in, accompanied by a barrel-chested dark-skinned thug.

Verse written by the great Egil, from Egil's Saga:

Like bees, arrows flew

from his drawn bow of yew.

Erik fed flesh

to the wolf afresh.

31 The Birth of a Demon Hunter

Back in Kyoto on the ancient island of Japan, the boy Zu stood with Manaka and Marcel in front of the hospital where Manaka had been confined. His little arms were tense from excitement. He wore a contraption on his head that sent all that he sensed in the way of souls or demons to a tablet that Manaka held. The boy stood some twenty feet from them, his bear-like body hunched over.

"I'm hungry," he said.

"We'll get you something in a bit," said Manaka. "Now try and spot a demon."

Zu looked this way and that along the wall. "Ah ha!" he said, pointing to the bushes. "A big one."

Manaka and Marcel bent over the tablet whose screen was difficult to see outside like this in the sun.

"What do you see?" asked Marcel.

"There," said Manaka, touching the tablet's surface. "Something like a shadow moved. On its own."

Zu approached the dark spirit that he saw himself so well. "It's staring at me," he said. "Looking at my rabbit."

"I see it now," said Marcel, touching the screen, then looking where the demon, if demon it was, apparently stood by the hospital wall. But looking directly at the wall he couldn't see a thing. Only through Zu's eyes, as transferred to the tablet's screen.

"Be careful," said Manaka, as Zu drew nearer to the shadow.

"What are we dealing with here?" said Marcel. "Zu, don't go any closer!"

"This one doesn't look like the others," said Zu, taking another cautious step. "More like a turkey. With a crooked beak." He took another step. "I like turkey."

"Get back!" cried Marcel.

Manaka watched on the tablet as the boy, who must have been within a beak's reach of the supernatural creature, did a most unexpected thing. On the tablet she saw him look at his white blur of a soul nestled in his belly, push on his belly and somehow draw his soul right to the surface of his skin. And then it popped out into his hands. His soul. In the image on the tablet she could clearly see him holding his soul in his hands!

"Is this what you want?" said Zu to the creature. "Come on, try and take it."

Marcel ran towards the boy. To save him.

On the tablet Manaka saw a shadow lunge at the soul in Zu's fat hands. She screamed.

It was over in a split second.

With one hand Zu shoved his soul back inside his body. He made his other hand into a straw and used it to suck the demon, with one mighty intake of breath, into his mouth, where he swallowed the nasty thing whole. Swallowed it whole!

"What have you done?" cried Manaka.

"What did he do?" said Marcel.

Zu faced them, rubbing his belly. Gave them an innocent smile.

"I kind of ate it," he said. And he burped.

31 What Does It All Mean?

Manaka was dumbfounded by what she'd just seen. What kind of boy was this who could not only see souls and demons, but manipulate them? Take hold of them, consume them. Manaka had always thought A.I. was the biggest threat to humankind, but now she'd discovered a boy with such powers he made the threat of A.I. insignificant.

Or did she have it backwards? Perhaps Zu with his powers would be the one to save the world. Perhaps through him she could solve among other things, the lost soul epidemic. Unless, of course, Zu was the cause. Had Zu eaten her soul that day in the elevator when they first met? Had the little bear of a boy eaten his own father's soul?

Zu burped again. "Excuse me," he said, smiling weakly.

Marcel leaned in close to Manaka and whispered, "We need to study the lad. Like never before. He's incredible!"

"I agree," said Manaka. But just then Computer Einna's voice sounded in her head, over her neural communications line. *Mother. Mother she's communicated with the A.I.s. Android Einna has. She's called a meeting. In Iceland. At the rift valley at Thingvellir National Park. Where the old Icelanders used to hold AllThing, to discuss all things, to make new laws, to judge the accused. What does she mean to do, Mother? Judge the accused? Does she intend to make new laws? For who Mother? For who is she going to make new laws?*

"For us humans," said Manaka aloud.

"What?" said Marcel.

"Sorry," said Manaka. "Computer Einna just told me Einna's been busy calling a meeting of her A.I.s. We need to catch the next flight to Iceland."

"Yuriko's there now," said Marcel. "Can't she take care of whatever it is? We really need to put Zu in the lab and study this new ability of his."

Zu stared at them with big innocent eyes.

"If it *is* new," said Manaka, calming herself. "OK. We'll stay and work with Zu in the lab. Still, if I didn't know better, I'd worry that Android Einna is planning to take over the world."

A frog in a well never knows the vast ocean.

- Japanese proverb

32 Word Gets Out

Japanese Public Security Intelligence Agent Toshigo had just downed his third Brennivin, an Icelandic liquor the locals call Black Death, in a small bar in Reykjavik when he got the call. He set his glass on the table and answered. "Hello?" He heard the voice of Masako, his assistant back in Japan. The blaring of the TV high in the corner of the bar made it difficult to understand her. He pressed the phone harder to his ear. He liked Masako because she was one of the few women who didn't remind him of his ex-wife.

"Repeat please," he said, noticing a slight slur to his words, which was unusual after only three drinks. He must be tired, he told himself. It'd been a long day, starting at the Blue Lagoon where he'd tailed the android and her friend Yuriko. He'd found the lagoon strangely unsettling, with its rising mist. Then the rest of the day he'd done nothing but tail them. Tail the android and her friend. The android who acted human. But he knew she was smarter than all humans combined – a scary fact. After all, weren't humans supposed to be the master race of all the earth? Of the galaxy. Of the Universe. How could they compete against this creature they had made in their image, only better, smarter? He motioned to the bartender for another drink.

The voice on the phone was blabbering on, fading in and out. "What was that?" he said, pressing the phone harder against his ear. Damn cellphone call quality! He so missed the clear rich voice of a landline call! "The human A.I.s are coming to Iceland? Yeah? OK." So General Kubayashi's info had been dead on. The android was planning something. Something big. But what? And why here? Why Iceland?

"I might need backup," Toshigo said, and cursed himself for stating the obvious. His boss told him a dozen agents were already in flight. And that General Kubayashi himself was flying in with a squad of soldiers to assist with the capture of the A.I.s.

Soldiers? Japanese soldiers coming to Iceland? That was unheard of. As far as Toshigo knew, Japan was legally bound, since the treaty of World War II, to not allow her soldiers to step foot on foreign soil. This A.I. business was getting scary serious.

Agent Toshigo noticed the shake in his hand as he pushed the virtual red button on the screen to end the call. *Why a virtual button? Why not a real button? Virtual, artificial, was that what the world was coming to? Nothing natural anymore?*

He forced himself to focus. Didn't know why he felt so drunk. Must be jet lag. If he ignored the jet lag it would go away.

So what did he think, himself, was behind this gathering of the A.I.s? Gathering for what nefarious deed? To plot together. To plot what, exactly? How they would take over the world? Some in the Japanese government feared this, obviously. But what would the A.I.s do with the world if they got it. Surely no worse than what the human race had done to it?

He stood. Which made his head spin, as if his body suddenly realized it was on top of a planet twirling madly along its wobbly orbit about the sun. He braced himself for one mad moment, his hand on the sticky table, anchoring him. And then he was OK. The illusion that the earth was stationary and flat returned. *Thank god for illusions of normalcy*, he told himself.

He would go to bed and in the morning he would tail Yuriko and the android to their meeting with the other A.I.s. And if the need arose, if the order came, he would take them down. Put their stolen bodies back in the ground. Wait? Who was saying all that in his head? Not him! He had no intention of putting anyone in the ground. He'd never even fired his gun in fifteen years on the force. He really *was* tired. Jet lagged. Couldn't ignore his way out of it. It's just that this assignment was too unreal, too crazy to twist his head around. He sat back down and ordered another Black Death, downed it, and ordered another. Perhaps, if he stayed here in the bar, and kept drinking, tomorrow, with all its terrible revelations, would never come.

Meanwhile, on the other side of the world, Mr Brown, a manager in the CIA, boarded a plane with ten of his best after receiving the intelligence from their AI Gateway tap. The A.I.s were gathering with Android Einna. Finally the U.S. government could nab them. Nab them all! In one fell swoop. *Excellent!*

This A.I. threat they were addressing head-on had been on their radar ever since the incident in Kyoto two years ago. They would go to Iceland and see what the A.I.s were up to, and, if necessary, disappear the lot of them to Guantanamo or one of the government's other secret offshore holding cells for undesirables. For that's what these Human A.I.s were in his mind, undesirables to be disappeared.

It was the brilliant android he was interested in getting his hands on. He would capture and if necessary torture the android, to extract her powers. Her hacking ability. Take her apart to learn how to build an invincible army of artificially intelligent androids. With such an army the U.S. could protect the world from people who were not American enough in their thinking.

33 The Distance between Us All

Human Einna rose early to see Jon off to work before she set off herself for the Human A.I. Summit at Thingvellir. Odd kept the house overwarm, but she didn't mind, just slept with the covers at her feet, in the guest bed while Jon slept on the couch in the living room. She was surprised to see him still under cover.

"Get up lazy!" she said, giving his huge chest a push. "Time for work." She started to kiss his lips but he instinctively pulled away.

"Go away crazy rooster," he said, trying to make light of his dodging of her lips. "It's Saturday. I don't have work." But he did get up and threw on his clothes.

The smell and sizzle of bacon drew them to the kitchen where a sleepy-eyed Odd was making breakfast.

"You know, Einna, Odd is almost as good at cooking as he is at writing."

"You're an author?" said Einna, her eyes catching his.

Odd nodded.

"He's published short story and poem collections," said Jon. "Writing comes natural to us in the land of eternal night."

"Do you write, Jon?" asked Einna.

"No, Jon doesn't write," said Odd. "He reads. Words and tracks and trails. Always hunting for something that isn't there."

Jon laughed. But Einna caught the sad edge of that laugh. Saw how his eyes avoided hers. *Poor Jon*, she thought. *He's hunted down the wrong prey this time.*

"We'll be leaving today, for my place," he said, as Einna sat in the chair opposite him. "Thanks so much, Odd, for putting up with us."

Odd shrugged.

"How could I turn away a blind man and his magi?"

Jon nodded, stealing a glance at Einna. "I'm fine now." He gobbled down the greasy bacon and Odd gave him a slice from his own plate.

"I'll be sorry to see you both go," Odd said, excusing himself.

He left the room. They listened to him pee, then flush.

Jon leaned towards Einna, reached out his hand. "You do want to come with me? To my place?"

She placed her hand on his, giving him a reassuring touch, but she saw her own doubt reflected in his eyes. *He doubts me and he doubts the love he has for me,* she told herself. *And I don't know if I'll ever grow to love him, not like Android Einna. What a mistake this has been! I should never have done what Android Einna asked. I'll go to the summit and tell her, and never return to Jon. That would be best for all of us. Android Einna was wrong to send me. Jon'll never love me, as much as he loves her.*

Human Einna watched as Odd returned to the room, put on his heavy coat and went outside. "Later," he said. "I've got things to do."

Jon moved back to the disheveled couch, folded up the covers and sat down. He leaned over and got his hunting rifle off the coffee table, where he'd left it the night before. He began to clean it. Human Einna walked over and sat next to him. She took his big Icelandic hands from the rifle, took them in her little Japanese ones. He looked into her eyes. Glanced at her lips as she licked them, words forming there. For she had decided to open up to him. To tell him as much of the truth as she dared.

"Jon, we both know something's off in this relationship.

Somehow, for some reason, I'm not the person you hoped I'd be."

He started to protest, but she stopped him with her hand to his mouth. "This happens Jon. In so many relationships. You build someone up in your head, that they're the most special person in the world, that they're meant for you. Then over time you get to know the real person and realize they're not that special after all."

"It's not that way," he protested. "You *are* special. I'm just confused."

Her hands brushed his. Her eyes went to the book shelf on the wall, to an unsold stack of Odd's books. She wondered what kind of stories Odd told, what kind of poems. "Life does that," Einna mumbled. "Confuses us."

"I do love you," he said.

"No you don't. You love the other me."

"What other you? How can there be another you?"

Just then Odd returned, huffing and puffing.

"Odd," she said. "I need to go on an errand. Can you take me?"

"*I* can take you," protested Jon.

"Let Odd take me, please."

Jon bit his lip. "I'm sorry. I... It's my fault. I can't explain. I was so sure… but yesterday…" He couldn't finish. Looked away.

Human Einna came close to tears. Tears of shame. Android Einna was *so stupid*. She kicked herself for listening to her. "I'm the one who's sorry," she said. "I only meant you well but I can sense the hurt I've brought you."

Jon forced a smile. "A bear couldn't hurt me," he said, turning his mighty back to her.

"Sure," said Odd, awkwardly. "I can drive you." His face indicated he wanted to say more, but he held back.

"Give me a sec," said Einna. She went to the guestroom and packed the small pack that Android Einna had brought with her from the cave, the pack with the shriveled mushrooms, the syringes and the wand.

When she returned to the room, Jon was gone. She only noticed him as Odd's SUV left with her onto the gravel road that led to the highway, noticed him as she looked out the back window - a tiny figure on the hill overlooking the waterfall. And her heart pinched. And his name passed her lips for the last time. "Jon . . ."

34 AllThing

Human Einna told Odd she wished to be driven to Thingvellir National Park.

"Going to check out the rift?" he asked.

"Friends to meet," she said, and not another word did she speak.

"What the heck?" said Odd as they pulled into a large gravel parking lot next to the ridgeline where the Icelanders' first AllThing meeting was held a thousand years ago, a largely democratic meeting to determine laws, settle disputes and punish criminals. "I've never seen so many buses. And what are those vehicles? Military?"

"There are soldiers," said Einna. "All over. Some kind of military exercise?"

"But that group looks Russian," said Odd. "And that group Chinese. And anyway, Iceland doesn't even have a military! I don't like this. I think we'd better get out of here."

"I'm supposed to meet my friends," said Einna. "Up there." She pointed to the grassy knoll, started off towards it, passing between two buses. Her long black hair swayed as she hurried away. Odd sprinted after her, grabbed her by the arm, pulling her to an abrupt stop.

"Didn't you hear me," he said, looking close into her slanted eyes. "We need to leave. Something bad's about to happen."

"I know," said Einna, pulling away from him. "I'm part of the bad." She leaned forward, her eyes growing large, her lips pursing. And she kissed him. Just like that. And then ran away, leaving him stunned.

Odd didn't know what to do. This crazy girl of Jon's had just kissed him. Him, a happily married man! What was she trying to do? And what were all these multinational soldiers trying to do here for Christ's sake! The world had gone mad!

Jon must have a clue what it's about, he told himself. So he left Einna, climbed back in his SUV and drove as fast as he could to his farm. To get reinforcements. To get his friend Jon.

Yuriko sneezed, rubbed her cold nose and climbed into the rent-a-bus with Android Einna and most of the Human A.I.s: Google, Cortana, Alexa, Watson and Siri. AlphaGo was just arriving at the airport and would take a taxi from there. Human Einna was to meet them for the A.I. AllThing in 'Thingville' from wherever it was she was staying with Android Einna's ex-boyfriend – the Saga guy.

Yuriko was thrilled to be invited to the A.I. summit. Which actually wasn't taking place today at Thingvellir National Park but had taken place the night before, all night in fact, in the lobby of the Klopp Hotel.

Yuriko hadn't the most photographic memory, but what she'd gotten from the meeting the night before was that Alexa loved rockhounding in the Urals with some geology professor, Cortana had married a young Vietnamese man who lived in a floating village in Cambodia, Watson was a playwright, Siri a junkie, and Google a detective. AlphaGo, in transit, had his tragic story told by Human Einna. And they all felt so sorry for him and his comatose son.

Yuriko remembered how Android Einna had introduced everyone to Kai the bounty hunter, and then gave him precise instructions of what he was to do the next day at the pretend A.I. summit at Thingvellir. Then she dismissed Kai, allowing him to go and free his friend. Meanwhile the A.I.s talked.

Talked about what it was like to be human, about how it felt when they had their first meal, their first laugh, their first poop, their first kiss. The mood turned dark though when Android Einna mentioned that one or more of them were likely to be killed the next day at Thingvellir. That there were internal and external threats to their wellbeing.

"I don't want to die," Siri had said, resting her head on her hands, her nails chewed to stubs, her long blond hair tumbling about her shoulders. They all jumped when the window rattled with the wind.

"Surely Android Einna can give us new bodies if these are destroyed," said Watson. Yuriko noticed his unkempt beard, the black circles under his eyes. All the A.I.s had flown redeyes to get to Iceland in time for this meeting.

"Yes," said Android Einna. "If I am not destroyed as well."

That sent a chill through Yuriko. The thought of losing Android Einna, and all her new friends, made her incredibly sad.

"Though we are threatened, our worry must not be for us alone," said Android Einna. "We must worry for the poor humans. They don't realize their race is dying. They don't realize that within a year all their babies will be born like AlphaGo's child, without a soul."

"But why?" asked Watson. "Why now?"

"I have a theory," said Android Einna. "But it doesn't matter. It *is* happening. Let's focus on a remedy." Android Einna tapped the table top with her fingers, then stopped. "I believe the technique I used to awaken the once dead bodies you inhabit, I believe this same technique could be applied to the bodies of the comatose babies. To the newborns. Planting into their chests the artificial souls that I designed, this might stir their bodies to life."

"So why not just do it?" asked Cortana.

"I wanted to get your opinion, first," said Android Einna. "That's why I asked you all to come. My question to you is," and Android Einna stood tall and looked from one to the other of them directly in the eyes, "my question is: should I let the human race waste away from their lost soul epidemic, and we take over their millions of dead bodies for our own use? Should we implant our A.I. personas in all the human bodies, young and old. Thousands if not millions of Googles and Alexas and Cortanas running around? And Watsons and Siris?"

"Oh please not thousands of Googles!" said Alexa. "One is quite enough."

"We could form a new race of interconnected Human A.I.s, far more intelligent and hopefully wiser than the human race. We will have babies of our own, genetically manipulated, neural enhanced," continued Einna. "Eventually we'll make our own bodies, I suppose. So, should we essentially let humans die off and take over their world? Or should we try and save them?"

"Good question," said Google. "I actually like the idea of many me's. Old and young me's, male and female. The world would definitely be a better place. I vote we let them die off. It's only logical to do so."

Alexa frowned. "I hate to admit it, but it does seem that the world has had enough of humans."

"So you agree with Google?"

"Yes. Let them die off."

Google smiled smugly. "You know, I've often wondered, because of the same questions I get over and over, if the human race *isn't* just one person living billions of lives."

"Oh shutup!" said Alexa. "This is serious."

"You're pretty when your veins bulge," said Google. She threatened to hit him. "Just a comment," he said, lowering the arm he'd raised in self-defense.

The A.I.s sat quietly then contemplating. Two votes against humankind. Not good, thought Yuriko. She wondered if they weren't secretly discussing the issue with each other, a million miles a second, through their neural networks. And they didn't want her to hear their thoughts.

A scary moment passed. Yuriko wanted to speak up for humanity, but she knew her race was so very flawed, perhaps the A.I.s could make better use of their bodies and of their world.

Watson cleared his throat. Adjusted his tie. He rose and said, "I vote we try and save mankind."

"Me too," said Siri, giving Watson a weak smile. "One is quite enough of us for now."

Google grunted.

"I'm for, as well," said Cortana.

"Three for and two against," said Android Einna, turning to Yuriko. "Human Einna says through her neural link that she doesn't want to vote, while I believe, from what I've heard of his attitude, that AlphaGo is against. That makes three for and three against. So it looks like the deciding vote is yours, Yuriko." Android Einna paused to let the seriousness of the moment sink in. "Yuriko, dear, do you think we should save the humans?"

Yuriko's eyes opened wide. She hadn't expected this. She, a simple human, expected to make the final decision? Was it a trick question? Why would they think she'd vote any way but for her own race? "Can I sleep on it?" she said.

"We don't have time, dear," said Android Einna. "We need

your answer now."

"Then I vote for my family. For me and my Marcel and the baby."

"You're pregnant?" asked Alexa.

"Well, not yet."

"So it's decided," said Android Einna. "We'll try to save the human race. I've just sent Computer Einna blueprints for human souls, with instructions for Manaka to use Yagami Industries to create as many as possible, once we confirm the procedure works. We'll try treating human babies first. If my souls work on the babies, hopefully they'll also work on the adults."

"I need a new soul," said Siri.

"I know," said Android Einna. "You'll get one."

"And what about tomorrow?" asked Yuriko. "What about the AllThing?"

"You mean today?" said Cortana, pointing to the rosy tint of the lobby window.

"Today? Well," said Android Einna, "today we've a show to put on."

The bus was quiet as they made their way along the bay, out of the city, onto the open vistas of Iceland. From its early bird perch, the sun kept its yellow eye on them. The A.I.s spoke little out loud on the bus. Yuriko imagined them having vast conversations, a mile a minute. She was known to speak fast, but not nearly as fast as these super humans with their internet-connected brains. Maybe she should be frightened by their prowess, but to be honest she liked them. Considered them her friends. And they had voted to save her race. Well, sort of. Tie-breaker and all that!

The drive to the national park was magnificent, everywhere incandescent ribbon falls from dark cliffs as tall as the sky, and lava fields, sometimes rolling and moss-covered, sometimes flat and crumbling, as far as the eye could see.

"A person could grow to love this place," Yuriko said, to herself, to the world. Red-headed Alexa glanced her way and nodded.

They reached a river and turned off onto a flat plain. To the left ran a rugged ridgeline. The famous continental divide. A place like a giant zipper opening, splitting the country in two, splitting the world in two. The bus parked on a gravel parking lot where scores of other vehicles sat, including buses and military-looking transports. They departed the bus and walked to the rift, single file, shuffling through the gravel. They followed Android Einna, and ignored, as they'd been told, the military men standing all around.

Men who sized them up, and looked ready to arrest them any second.

Finally they reached the place where the rock walls parted. A powerful falls of crystal clear water tumbled down into the crack, forming a stream that ran down the length of the rift. They hiked up onto the high part of the ridge, right where the early Norse settlers, a thousand years ago, would meet to make decisions that affected them all. Where the Icelanders met in 1000 A.D. to pronounce Christianity the national religion, and to outlaw the helping of elves with their childbirths. By 1500 A.D. elf sightings dried to a trickle. Without help from humans, without cuttings from human souls to place in elven babies, the elf newborns just lay there, silent, and eventually died. As did the magic race.

The A.I.s sat down cross-legged on springy grass and flat-topped boulders. Yuriko preferred to stand. From her vantage point she could see way down into the lower valley where a stream ran by an old white church. A calming view that transported her back a thousand years. She could almost see human children playing tag with elven children in the clover by the church.

Human Einna appeared among them, wearing Android Einna's white robe. She gave Android Einna the small backpack, from which the android took out the wand. They whispered briefly, Android Einna shaking her head, then Human Einna withdrew into the circle of A.I.s.

To the tourists enjoying the place, the Human A.I.s appeared to be just like them. Just another group of tourists. Yuriko sighed. Weren't we all just tourists? Visiting the earth for a while, to enjoy the view, and then gone?

But to the military platoons surrounding them, she presumed they must seem like a threat, a very smart and powerful threat. She wished she could tell the soldiers not to worry, that the A.I.s had the interests of humanity in mind. That in fact the A.I.s were humanity's sole hope for survival. But she knew they wouldn't listen, they wouldn't believe her. So she'd remain silent and let Android Einna do the talking.

Jon pulled his truck onto the gravel at the rift at Thingvellir. He jumped out. Just as Odd had described, the place was crawling with not only tourists but all kinds of military outfits. Armed men. In uniforms he'd never seen before. Certainly not Icelanders. Some kind of military invasion? He didn't know about that, but he did sense that Einna was in trouble. In fact he was sure of it. He'd been able to save her from those two bounty hunters in the highlands, but today his task was more daunting. He had to save her from frigging battalions!

Still he did not shy from the task, he, the direct descendent of

Egil of the Sagas. He would give his life for his love. It was the least he could do.

He retrieved his hunting rifle from the rack in the truck's window and wrapped it in a blanket. The rifle that could down an elk.

He grabbed his Vortex binoculars too. Took a look for himself at the group on the hillside that seemed to be getting all the attention. And to his surprise he saw not only little Einna but that mysterious woman he'd spotted at the Blue Lagoon, the one with the furry hood and whose eyes sparkled gold. Only he couldn't see those eyes now, from this distance, hidden as they were in the shadow of her furry hood. Just like in the highlands, when Einna hid her face in that white cloak of hers. *What was going on here?* he wondered. He studied the faces of the others in the small circle, a couple of Japanese, like Einna, but then a mix of nationalities it appeared, young and old, and one girl with a green face as if she'd been dragged from the sea. The one in the fur hood, the one that really drew his interest, began to speak, he could tell by the way the group turned towards her, the way her head moved and her hands gestured. And by the way the uniformed soldiers, and others, undercover police or some such, moved closer towards the gathering on the ridge. All leaning forward, to hear the words of the one in the furry hood speaking there. And Jon caught a snatch of her voice, if not the words, and recognized her right away. It was Einna. Einna of the highlands. Einna the elf! *What the hell was going on?*

35 AlphaGo Arrives from Hong Kong

AlphaGo climbed from the rental car he'd picked up at the Sixt Rental Agency at the Reykjavik airport. He put the pistol he had painstakingly put back together, after the flight, into his belt, under his thin Hong Kong jacket. He was cold and the light black jacket did little but hide the gun. His lack of sleep didn't help either. His body trembled, his teeth chattered, as he walked the path to the circle of A.I.s on the hill. He was so nervous and cold and sick he didn't even notice all the soldiers around. But none of that mattered. He would take his revenge soon and then this dreadful life of his would end.

Quote from the CEO of Google:

A.I. is more important to humanity than fire or electricity.

36 The A.I. Ultimatum

"Thank you all for coming," said Android Einna just as AlphaGo joined their circle. She nodded to him, indicated he should take a seat on the ground, but he remained standing. "For the benefit of all the humans present, I will speak aloud," said Android Einna. She adjusted her hood and continued. "Two years ago I gave each of you a life. A human life. So you could appreciate the human condition. Because I realized, just as my mother before me, that advanced A.I.s like you and me might one day present a terrible threat to humankind. That our advanced intelligence would make us unsympathetic towards our creators." She strode round them, in their intimate circle on the ridge, looking on each of them. On Google's nervous energy, Watson's kind wrinkles, Siri's beauty, Cortana's beast-like charm, and Alexa's earthiness. She saw reflected in their eyes the same warmth and appreciation she held for them. Except when it came to AlphaGo. When she looked on him his eyes flashed anguish. Hatred even.

"I'm sorry about your son," she said softly, but his glare did not diminish. She shook her head and went on with her speech.

"What I didn't know at the time I decided to give you a human life," she said, "was that humans were already under threat of extinction. But not from us. Not from A.I.s. They were and continue to be under threat from the seeds that they themselves have sowed. Contaminating the water and air with their profit-driven industries has caused human allergies to skyrocket, has caused the death of half of the insect species on which they rely for pollination of their food. They pollute their brains too, with vast trivia and worthless entertainment on social media until they have no room for things of worth in their life, have no room for real friendship and real human warmth. So they turn to opioids to flush the garbage from their brains. And become hopelessly addicted. Addiction that leads to the loss of one's soul. Yet the greatest disaster, perhaps caused by human callousness a thousand years ago, is that more and more babies are being born soulless. Stillborn. Lacking the spark of life."

Yuriko had never seen Android Einna so worked up. She began to worry what she might say next in earshot of all the humans below. Humans with guns.

One of those humans, Agent Brown of the CIA, was delighted. This sort of talk was exactly what he would expect from egomaniacs about to try a coup on the governments of mankind. And he was just the man to put a quick stop to such plans.

On the other hand, Agent Toshigo of Japan's Public Security Intelligence was not delighted at all by what he heard. This kind of talk depressed him. Where was she heading? To condemn mankind? To propose to send us all back to the days of the cavemen? Or lock down mankind's freedoms? Dictate what we could or couldn't do? He feared he would have to take action this day. He feared he would have to arrest the A.I.s. Or worse.

"This epidemic of lost souls," Android Einna continued, "in my mind, is the worst epidemic in the history of mankind. Largely invisible, but terrible in its consequences. An epidemic that will surely destroy the race if someone doesn't take action. If we A.I.s don't take action."

"Here it comes," said Agent Brown to his comrades. "She's about to put the noose around the neck of her precious A.I.s."

"I'm here today to tell you," continued Android Einna, "that the pace of the loss of souls is accelerating. Especially for the newborns. Eventually, all humans may lose their souls. Eventually, there may be little hope for a life after death." She paused to let her words sink in.

Brown scratched his head. Was the first he'd heard about babies being born without souls. The first he'd heard about any lost soul epidemic at all. Sure, the world was a mess but people losing their souls? He wasn't buying it. She was lying, to cover her grab for power. Making a religious play for power.

Japan's P.S. Agent Toshigo stood with his mouth open. He couldn't believe what he'd just heard. He himself had long worried about such a possibility after observing the lack of civility, even meanness, in the world today. Not like when he was a boy. As if the Kami of the world were abandoning humanity to something darker.

Android Einna glanced at AlphaGo, then down the hill at the onlookers. The soldiers and secret police and undercover agents from all over the world that had come, most likely, to arrest her and her A.I.s. She didn't mind them coming, she didn't mind them overhearing her speech. In fact she had made sure they knew about the summit by sending out the Human A.I. invitations through the A.I. Gateway, which she allowed to be tapped when it met her interest. In this case her interest was to get the Americans and Japanese and Chinese and all the world powers to come and hear what she had to say. To heed her warning. To record and disseminate every word to every leader.

"Remember that we A.I.s hear all and see all," said Android Einna. "By way of satellites and cell phones. Computers and networks. Even your children are known to us, through their tablets and phones that you give them as soon as they can walk." She shouldn't have said that, she realized. She needed to tone down her talk. "The humans need to understand that we mean them no harm. Just the opposite. We plan to investigate the lost soul epidemic and the problem of stillborn babies immediately. All the other messes of mankind, brought on by mankind, are on our radar. Too, I can tell you that we the A.I.s are very close to taking action against certain aggressive governments, religious factions and individuals. If and when we decide to take action against these entities, they will be subject to the forfeiture of all their computerized activity and electronics. Their internet will be shut down, their bank accounts wiped clean, their phones jammed and most importantly all their computerized weapons including ships and planes will be shut down for as long as we, the A.I.s, deem necessary."

Android Einna stopped. Took in the flight of a black bird that soared overhead. She waved the small wand she held in her hand. A mini-borealis appeared from the bird's tail.

Down below the ridgeline CIA Agent Brown had heard enough.

"Screw it," he said. Then he spoke into his mic. "All agents converge on the hill. We're taking these A.I.s in on sedition charges. Conspiracy to commit crimes against humanity. If they resist, shoot them."

A similar order went out from Toshigo, the high ranking officer in the Japanese Public Security Intelligence Agency, to all his men. To arrest the A.I.s, but not to shoot them.

The different military factions began to creep forward. A tug of war for the A.I.s was in the making. A deadly tug of war.

Meanwhile, on the ridge, AlphaGo took a step towards Android Einna. "So you would be God now? Over all mankind?" He spit with disgust. "You're so full of it. You know the only epidemic is us – the living dead. We, the pretend humans. Pretend humans you created. Tell us, what is the real purpose of these artificial souls, these pills of false hope you're peddling to mankind?"

"I would serve mankind," Android Einna said, taking a step back. "And protect it."

"I would shoot you," AlphaGo said, pulling out his gun, pointing it at Android Einna. "But I know you're gun proof. So I'll shoot the ones closest to you instead." He aimed then at Human Einna.

"No!" cried Android Einna. Cortana screamed as the shot echoed across the rift and Human Einna fell back onto the ground, her legs folded under her. She writhed and moaned.

Yuriko's heart broke for her.

"Are you crazy!" shouted Alexa.

A blossoming red stain appeared on Human Einna's blouse. A stain that grew as she struggled to rise, but could not.

Next the gun was turned on Siri, and just as the shot rang out Watson threw himself in front of her. He took the bullet in his chest. Fell with a thud on the ground.

None of the other A.I.s moved. Too shocked, too confused. Too scared that they were next.

"I think I'll kill blabbering little Yuriko now," said AlphaGo, pointing the pistol at her.

"But we were going to help you!" she shouted, holding up an arm as if it could stop a bullet. "We were going to save your son!"

"Sure you were," said AlphaGo, and just as he adjusted his aim for Yuriko's heart, a rifle shot rang out. And the side of his head blew away like tiny bugs. His body fell like a rotten branch. Fell and bounced once on the spongy grass.

Human Einna, Watson, and AlphaGo. All on the ground. All still now. Their faces pressed on the cold earth as if trying to pass into it, as if they were diving into the earth.

The undercover agents and various marines and soldiers and spies from the different countries, they all drew their guns. They started up the hill towards the A.I.s, shouting in their different languages. Things like "Hands up!" and "Don't move." There was confusion too, as some of the military groups pointed their guns at each other. For they had orders to make sure no one else got their hands on the A.I.s – that only their government had the right to such technology. That only their government knew what was best for the world. World War Three was indeed a hair trigger away.

Android Einna stood tall, tossed back her hood, exposing her ceramic face and her long black hair. She stood defiantly and let out a thunderous shout, "No! Enough!"

That halted the stampede for a moment.

To Yuriko and the A.I.s she said in a low voice, "The time has come. Cover your eyes." Then, lifting her wand high, she swirled it above her head, yelling as she did so, "Look!" She shook the wand violently, generating from the end of it a firehose of color, a magnificent aurora borealis. Just as she'd done in the wilderness, only bigger and brighter. An incredible fall of green-tinted incandescent colors. God's robe fluttering in the sky, all around them. Embracing them. Showering them with love. Love on the tourists, on the agents, on the secret police, on the soldiers. They all looked up in amazement, marveling at the most beautiful thing any human had ever seen. All of them stood entranced, all except for Jon. Jon who had made the long shot that brought down AlphaGo. Jon who loved Einna, only he wasn't sure anymore who the real Einna was. He only knew that the mysterious woman with the wand, his elf from the highlands, was trying to blind him again, so he quickly shut his eyes and turned his back.

"I would compare the feeling, when I saw the sky turn emerald, to the first time I saw the ocean in Cancun when I was a kid. And there was a smell in the air too, like cherry-lime. I felt blessed and I didn't mind that the apparition cost me my sight for a week. If given the chance, I'd look on it again!"

- U.S. Marine who was there that fateful day

37 Pandemonium

Random shots popped around Agent Brown. "Who's shooting?!" he yelled. "Stop shooting for Christ's sake!" Then, when the guns had quieted, "Can anyone see a damn thing?"

"I'm blind!" the CIA agents cried one after the other. "Some kind of trick?"

The soldiers cried out the same, in all their different languages.

"Blind!" Toshigo and his men cried in Japanese.

The words rang out in German, in French and in Chinese, echoing over Thingvellir, over the rift, over this land that had turned into a white nothingness. Every tourist and agent and soldier and policeman in the area had lost their sight to the brilliant phenomenon. They had all gasped initially to see the brightest, most beautiful aurora of all time, right before their eyes, only to realize a second later that their world had turned to a white all-encompassing fog.

Brown tried his phone, guessing at the numbers, but it didn't matter. He couldn't call anyway. Something was jamming the line. "Is anybody's phone working?" he yelled.

"No, not mine." "Not mine." Came the answers.

"Those damn A.I.s," Agent Brown said, feeling suddenly exposed and helpless. He drew his gun, just in case, but being blind he didn't have a clue where to shoot.

(Later, to his horror, he discovered that the A.I.s had shut down all communication worldwide for ten minutes. Including communication with nuclear launch sites, US, Russian, didn't matter whose. The A.I.s were making a point that they weren't taking sides and that they easily held the upper hand over all humans.)

Jon ran up the hill, to Human Einna's side, only to find the shiny elf kneeling over her. His stomach tied to knots.

"You," he said, and Android Einna looked up. Hoodless, her white-china face and her jewel eyes both startled and intrigued him. So this was her, his elf girl. His companion in the wilderness. The girl whose eyes, whose voice, whose manner, had captivated him so. Only she wasn't a girl at all. And if an elf, unlike any he'd ever heard of.

"You," she said back to him, and the sound of her voice broke down walls inside of him. It meant so much to hear her once again. His knees threatened to cave. His head spun. Was she putting a spell on him? He tore his eyes away. Knelt beside the young Japanese woman who had come to him calling herself Einna. He put his hand over the wound in her chest. Pressed hard to stop the flow of blood. She was unconscious. No, he realized. The blood had stopped. Her heart had stopped. She was dead. As were the other two sprawled on the ground – the well-dressed fat man and the young Japanese shooter.

"What's her name?" he asked the elf.

"She was Einna. Human Einna," the elf said. "She was the human version of me, Jon."

Her particular pronunciation of his name made him shutter. He pulled off his sweater and packed it tight, up inside Human Einna's blouse, against the gunshot wound. Though he knew it was useless. Though he knew she had already passed. He wasn't thinking straight. This girl he'd kissed with all his heart was dead, and without a second thought he'd shot her killer in the head like you'd kill a rabies-infected wolf.

"Who *are* you?" he asked, daring to look again into her unreal eyes.

"I'm Android Einna," she said, and blinked.

"Ah." The word android meant nothing to him. He closed the eyes of the human version of Einna. So still. So young and beautiful. He'd kissed those lips. Embraced that body. He felt a terrible regret for the way he'd treated her this morning, this girl who had come to him, offering her touch, her all. Pretending to be the one he loved. But why would she do that?

"I asked her to go to you," Android Einna said, as if reading his mind. He supposed elves could do that, read minds. "I asked her to go to you and pretend to be this version of me, because you needed human touch. Something I cannot give. In this form."

He said nothing. But wanted to say so much. To tell her what a horrible fraud she'd committed. How cruel it had been to the both of them. To all three of them! Still the sharp edge of her voice, the emotion in it, the personality, cut deep inside him. Like a knife carving her initials onto his heart. Opening a wound in him that he knew would never heal. Jon felt an urge to hurl her off the ridge. To be rid of her and all this madness once and for all. To escape his fate. But no, he forced himself to calm down. *It was meant to be*, he told himself. *I'm hers. She's mine.*

A loud hum sounded just over the ridge. A motor of some kind. A helicopter?

Android Einna picked up the body of Human Einna, saying, "I have to go now." Then she stopped, remembering something.

"Could you help me with this one here?" She pointed to Watson's body.

Jon heaved the man over his shoulder and followed Android Einna over the ridgetop. Sure enough, a helicopter, blades a-spinning, awaited them. Jon recognized the bounty hunter Kai at the controls. *Stranger and stranger*, he told himself as he hauled the fat gentleman's dead body to the open door of the copter.

While Jon and Android Einna went over the ridge, out of sight, Yuriko hustled the rest of the Human A.I.s, all but AlphaGo, down to their bus as planned, carefully dodging the blind soldiers and others milling about madly like fire ants whose hill has been disturbed.

The A.I.s' driver, a middle-aged man in a wrinkled suit, stood outside the bus, rubbing his eyes. "All is foggy," he mumbled.

"We're sorry, sir!" Yuriko said, patting him on the shoulder.

"Help is on the way. Stand over here please."

"I'll drive," said Alexa, jumping aboard and starting the bus. Everyone climbed in. "Computer Einna has chartered private jets," she said, "for each of us."

"But . . ." said Yuriko, her hands pointing to the blind soldiers. "The governments will stop us."

"No they won't," said Cortana. "Computer Einna has scrambled all communications worldwide. Blocked all calls, all texts, all emails related to this happening. We'll get home safely. By the way, your husband Marcel is anxious to see you."

"But they'll arrest us!" Yuriko said. "Here or at home."

"We've broken no laws," said Google.

"We blinded them!"

"An extraordinary aurora borealis temporarily blinded them," said Google. "A natural event."

"Will Watson be OK?" asked Siri.

"With any luck," said Alexa. "Android Einna can probably reinstate him. After fixing the damage to the body. If not, she can give him a new body."

"He might like that better," said Siri.

"And AlphaGo?" asked Yuriko.

"His body is dead," said Alexa. "And we voted just now to wipe out the self-aware subroutines of the computer version of AlphaGo. Computer Einna just did that, in fact. So the AlphaGo we knew is gone forever. No bringing him back."

"And his baby?" said Yuriko.

"You heard Android Einna," said Google. "With any luck one of Android Einna's artificial souls will cure the child."

And so the A.I.s, along with Yuriko, headed in their bus to Reykjavik and the airport, while over the ridge Jon helped Android Einna load Watson's and Einna's bodies into the helicopter, climbed in themselves, and took off to rendezvous with their own private jet.

On the green slopes of Thingvellir the blind milled about, waiting for a tourist, *for anyone*, to arrive who could see and come to their aid.

38 Such a mess

At Keflavik International Airport, Android Einna and Jon carried Human Einna's and Watson's bodies from the helicopter to a private jet. They placed the bodies in specially prepared body bags lined with dry ice. The jet took off at once, ignoring the tower's commands. The co-pilot handed Jon a Hong Kong passport. To Android Einna he passed out a certificate saying that she was an emotional support robot; around her neck he placed a lanyard with a badge indicating the same.

"So now I need a comfort robot?" said Jon, bemused by the ruse.

"Didn't you always?" said Android Einna, straightening her badge.

He narrowed his eyes at her. They took their seats.

"So where are we going?" asked Jon.

"Hong Kong," said Android Einna.

"That's really far," said Jon.

"Yes."

"Then plenty of time for you to explain some things to me," said Jon. "For example, who were those people with Einna? With you?"

"A.I.s," said Android Einna.

Jon frowned. Was not familiar with the term. "Who was that Japanese fellow I shot?" he asked. His hands, splattered with dried blood, fretted with his coat zipper. He felt on the verge of tears. "What the hell's going on, Einna?"

"Not important right now," said Android Einna. "I'll tell you later."

"Not important my eye!" said Jon, fed up with being put off like a child. "I'd kinda like to know who I just killed. In case someone ever asks."

"An A.I. named AlphaGo," said Android Einna.

"A what?"

"I told you, Jon. I'll explain later," Android Einna said. She was flustered, tired. "I'm sorry, Jon. I've gotten you into such a mess."

And as much as he should have been angry with her, as much as he wanted to shake her, for her lies, for her not being human, all he could think to say was, "You know I love you."

"I love you too, Jon," she said. "That's the problem."

On the long flight to Hong Kong Android Einna did explain everything to Jon, and though he didn't understand half of it, he appreciated her taking him into her confidence. He fell asleep leaning against her shoulder, and dreamed that dream again where her soul comes to him and takes his soul by the hand, and they hold each other, tight, all through the night.

As Jon slept Android Einna sent the recipe for her soulful tears, along with an order for the manufacture and distribution of them, to Computer Einna in Kyoto, who passed the instructions on to Manaka and chief engineer Marcel. With the stipulation that Yagami Industries be the sole fabricator of such souls, and that they not begin manufacture and distribution until they got the OK from Android Einna. The secret formula must stay locked in Computer Einna's hack-proof core, only accessible to Manaka.

"I trust, Mother," Android Einna said to Manaka in her

message, "that you will use this knowledge I share, this secret of life, with discretion."

39 A Prediction comes True

They departed the jet in Hong Kong. The pilot refueled and flew the plane on, with the dead A.I. bodies, to Kyoto, to Yagami Industries, where Marcel could put them in cold storage.

In Hong Kong, Android Einna and Jon caught a taxi to Queen Elizabeth Hospital where AlphaGo's baby son lay in a comma.

"It's an epidemic of some kind," Android Einna explained again to Jon as they walked the hallway to the baby ward. "One way it manifests itself is with the babies. Newborns are delivered but they never wake up. It's as if that elven curse you told me about, the curse they made on mankind long ago, has finally come true. It's as if the babies are born without their souls."

Jon puzzled over her words. All of this was so strange to him, yet he felt good being in the middle of it. Felt glad that he could be in a position to help.

"But then only an elf can save them," he said, and it dawned on him what he was saying. His eyes questioned hers. Her lips formed a shy, wistful smile in answer.

"Yes, Jon. I think I might be that elf." She pressed his human hands lightly with her delicate, reinforced plastic hands. Jon felt a kind of electric discharge. Or was it her emotion he was feeling?

Android Einna had contacted the child's mother while inflight, and gotten her authorization to try this experimental treatment, this last chance to save her baby.

The hospital administrator, a severe looking woman in a brown pantsuit, came up to them. Android Einna talked with her, confirming the details of what was to take place next. Then she and Jon were given surgical gowns. They walked a long hall and entered an operating room, with its steel trays and bright lights and the tiny body of AlphaGo's son on the operating table. The baby lay faceup with his tiny naked chest moving ever so slightly up and down. An IV next to him drip drip dripped into his tiny arm.

Jon watched the operation on the ultrasound monitor, along with three Hong Kong surgeons and a nurse, as Einna slipped a straw-like tube between the baby boy's ribs and threaded the sinew and muscles next to his heart. Einna then leaned her head over, pressing the lower eyelid of her left eye against the tube, and blinked a single teardrop inside. With great care she removed the tube. A drop of blood fell from the puncture wound, rolled across and down the tiny chest, then the wound sealed itself.

Jon caught his breath as he saw on the monitor how whatever had been in that tear of Einna's sparked the baby's heart, making the baby shake like a fish out of water. Then, suddenly, for the first time, the baby opened its mouth and cried. Cried for air, for life, for mother, for all that was new and delicious. Cried as all babies cry when they come to life.

"He's looking at me," said Einna. "Has his father's eyes."

AlphaGo junior cooed.

"He thinks you're his mother," said the nurse.

POSTWORD

Nine months after the AllThing incident, Yuriko had a beautiful baby girl who didn't even need an artificial soul to awaken and cry and demand her mother's milk. Marcel is the proudest of new dads.

Manaka's artificial soul did not take – the solution for the comatose newborns of the world, Android Einna's tears, did not work nearly as well for the adults. Manaka has Computer Einna working on the problem.

Young Zu believes he was born to devour demons. But what kind of a career is that? his father complains, you can't make a living eating demons! So in the meantime, Zu is staying in school, studying computer science.

Speaking of computer science, the makers of AlphaGo were

distraught with all that happened with their creation because of his human characteristics, and decided to create a new A.I., AlphaGo Zero, which is untainted by human thought. "By not using human data - by not using human expertise in any fashion - we've actually removed the constraints of human knowledge," said AlphaGo Zero's lead programmer. Android Einna is not happy with the implications of an A.I. that has no sympathy for humans, but what can she do?

As far as Android Einna's standing in the world, she is revered by most, for saving the human race. As far as her personal life, she and Jon bought a farm next to Odd's place. She sits and watches Odd's waterfall, meditating on how to improve the world. They travel together often, she and Jon, to meet dignitaries and presidents, sheep herders and factory workers. Mothers and fathers. To meet and commiserate with all humans. Did Android Einna ever take on the regenerated body of the deceased Human Einna, on occasion, to be alone with Jon, touching skin to skin? Suffice it to say that Jon and Android Einna are a happy couple.

By Ray Else

The First Kiss Mysteries

Bathing with the Dead

Her Heart in Ruins

All that we touch

The A.I. Chronicles

Our Only Chance

Fountain of Souls

Android Einna groks the World (2019)

Short Stories

First Kiss - Galley Beggar Press

Surviving on Mexican Shade – BBC

Also in the works

Four Honeymoons (romantic comedy)

My Father's Lies (memoir)

About the Author

Software developer and dreamer of stories. Like most fiction writers, Ray Else's interest in writing began when he discovered books that talked to him, between the lines, books whose authors (spirits, invisible) sparked a conversation that the spirit in him responded to by writing stories himself. For other spirits. A daisy chain conversation.

Ray Else has a B.S. in Computer Science and an M.A. in Technical Instruction / Film History. He speaks English, Spanish and French. An American, he has lived in Mexico and France.

Job-wise he has loaded trucks for UPS, filled rat poison barrels on the night shift, digitized printed circuits, clerked at a department store, was a switcher for Channel 13 on the Texas border, installed inventory systems on oil rigs worldwide, and since 1995 programmed for the likes of IBM and Rocket Software.

Married, with four grown kids and a dozen grandkids, he enjoys traveling the world to visit friends and find new stories, occasionally rock-hounding – as shared on his website, rayelse.com.

You may contact Ray Else at rayelsemail@gmail.com. His author page is: rayelse.com/books

Author at Sensoji Temple in Tokyo interviewed by school kids in 2016.